# Firestarter

# Patsy Collins

To my friend – Anne Rainbow Thomas

With gratitude for your time, support,
help, guidance and of course
your red pen!

## Chapter 1

Alice ran her fingers through her hair in case pulling the slinky dress over her head had caused static. Today her sister would have even less cause than usual to suggest she was turning into a frump. Alice couldn't think why she hadn't worn this dress before. The bright pink was a fab colour for her, just as Kate had said when she'd bought it.

'You look hot, Sis. Almost a fire hazard!'

'You think?'

An assistant had joined them then. 'It's perfect for you.'

Alice repeated her, 'You think?' but in a far milder tone.

'Yep. Of course as long as you show those legs you could probably get away with anything, but this style really works with curves and the colour is stunning against your olive skin and all that glossy hair.'

'Thanks.'

'That's what I was saying,' Kate said.

'No you didn't, you said I looked dangerous.'

'Fire hazard is what I said, cloth ears. Want me to dial 999 and get a fireman to talk you out of it in the interests of public safety?'

'No I don't and anyway, I'm totally over firemen.' She'd rushed back into the changing room before Kate could make a sarcastic comment.

The dress had hung in her wardrobe ever since, halfway between the size twelves she couldn't do up if she wanted to breathe and the size sixteens which gave her room to move, but no particular desire to strut her stuff. Tony had pointed out, quite correctly, that the snug fitting, scorchingly hot pink dress wasn't suitable for the office. It didn't seem suitable for any of the places he took her to either. Cool, understated elegance was the look he apparently preferred. All buttoned up, hemmed down crisp linen. Still, today she was going to the New Forest Show with her sister, not a wine bar with him. When he got an eyeful of her in this, he might want to rethink his conservative attitude. In fact she was positive this dress was just the thing to persuade him to loosen up a bit.

'Well, what do you think?' she asked as she half danced into her living room. She did a little twirl, then realised he hadn't so much as glanced up from his laptop.

'Tony, I'm going now.'

'Right.' He looked up. 'Oh, Alice, I thought we agreed that dress wasn't an appropriate item for you to wear.'

His tone was so cold he might as well have thrown a bucket of iced water over her. She'd suggested he do that for real when the charity craze had gone round, but he'd said it was childish and had simply made a donation. Alice and Kate, wearing bikinis, had soaked each other and the pictures when posted on the Internet had got quite a reaction.

Despite what Kate had said about the dress, there seemed to be no chance of Alice causing a fire around Tony, but he hadn't quite put out her spark.

'For work, or an evening out, maybe it isn't the best choice, but it's perfect for a hot summer day.'

'A day you'll be spending without me.'

'I asked if you'd like to come,' Alice said as calmly as she could.

'I can't just take a day off work.'

'Not now, but you could have when I first suggested it.' Trying not to show her anger, Alice headed for the door. He was the one who'd decided the project he and his colleague Rachel were working on was more important, so he'd be spending the day with his buttoned up, hemmed down, linen-clad colleague. A colleague who was slimmer, cleverer and classier than Alice. Really it was quite understandable that one of them had jealousy issues. What was less obvious to Alice was why it was Tony who was so distrustful.

'Wait a minute, Alice,' he called as she was about to slam the door to her flat.

Now what? Would he make himself late for work by walking her to the bus stop and ensuring it really was her sister she met?

'Take this.' He handed her a couple of twenty pound notes. 'Get yourself and Kate some lunch to keep your strength up for all that shopping and looking at animals or whatever it is you'll be doing.'

'Oh. Thanks.' She was heading for the door again when it occurred to her that wasn't a very gracious response to a rather sweet gesture. She went back and kissed his cheek. 'Say hi to Rachel for me and don't work too hard.'

'Right,' he said but his attention was already back on the screen of his laptop.


Getting the bus to the New Forest Show was part of the tradition. Alice and Kate had done it with their parents ever since the year it rained so heavily that cars had to be towed off the grass car parks with tractors at the end of the day. When their parents no longer wanted to arrive first thing and spend all day, they'd agreed Kate was old and sensible enough to take her little sister on the bus. They still went together.

On the journey the sisters studied the programme, taking note of entertainments they wanted to see. Kate penned a big tick against Hampshire Fire Service's demonstration.

'You didn't ask me,' Alice said.

'No need. You were moving so I could tell you weren't dead yet.'

'I told you already that I don't have a thing about firemen anymore.'

'Remember when you were six and ate all my Easter eggs and said it was the dog?'

Alice tried to look innocent, but knew she was no more successful than she had been twenty years previously. 'I should have said the goldfish did it, at least we had one of them.'

'My point exactly.'

'Eh?'

'Plausible deniability.'

'Eh again.'

'You're not demonstrating any, which is why I don't believe you.'

They pulled faces at each other, then returned to their study of the programme.

Alice's mobile buzzed to say she had an incoming text.

'Tony checking up on you already, is he?' Kate asked.

Ignoring her, Alice looked at her phone. The message was from Tony, saying he hoped she had fun and reminding her to photograph the eggs on plates.

'Why does he want to see them?' Kate asked, when Alice handed over her phone.

'He didn't believe it was a real thing.'

'Even I can't blame him for that, it is pretty mad.'

By the time they arrived at the, thankfully dry, show ground they had their day pretty well planned out. Just as they had since childhood they entered free competitions and charity raffles. They stroked Highland cattle, aaahed over spotted piglets and watched falconry, heavy horses and daring motor cycle displays.

Kate took plenty of photographs, including some of the rows and rows of paper plates, each with an egg cracked onto it.

'Honestly, how can anyone judge them?' Kate asked. 'They all just look like eggs.'

'Not at all, young lady,' said a man wearing red trousers and a moustache which looked like it should be on a lead. He explained, at length and in detail, what the differences were and how the egg laid by his own hen showed superiority not only in the colour of the yolk, but in the clarity and texture of the white.

'Thank you, that was most interesting, but we must go now,' Kate said the moment she could get a word in.

The sisters speed walked out, just managing to suppress their giggles until outside the poultry marquee.

'Right, where next?' Kate asked.

'Nowhere until you promise not to ask any more technical questions.'

'Oh, I promise. Double quadruple promise and hope to die.'

'OK then. Let's see if we can grab some freebies.'

They no longer collected every free pen, bag and silly cardboard hat they could get their hands on, but they did try a few samples of food and drink. Years of practice meant they managed to be in just the right position when the man demonstrating the toastie maker, or non-stick pans had food ready to distribute. They didn't compete to see who could pile the most mustard or jam onto a crumb of cracker as they once had, instead they tasted the various wines and spirits on offer. That was another reason for travelling by bus.

'No, not that one,' Alice said, pulling Kate away from a stand offering malt whisky.

'They do liqueurs. I fancy the one with raspberries and cream.'

'Me too, but later.' Alice urged her sister away. 'Miles is in there. I don't want to deal with him on my day off.'

'Which one is he?' Kate peered over Alice's shoulder.

'In the turquoise shirt.'

'He looks quite cute.'

'Kittens, baby bunnies and hunky, scantily clad firemen are cute. Nothing as slimy as Miles Molde could possibly be described that way.'

'Kittens, bunnies and what?'

'Er, yes... well even though I'm not especially keen on firemen, I do admit they're more appealing than my creep of a boss.'

'Anyone'd think you didn't like him.'

Alice, who'd often moaned to Kate about her moody boss, ignored that. 'Is drink tax deductible if it's for hospitality or something?'

'The companies must get an allowance for the samples.'

'I didn't mean them, I was thinking about Miles. He was buying loads of that stuff, but swears he can't afford to give us pay rises or repair the building.'

'If he buys whisky at £65 a bottle then I'm not surprised he can't.'

'And he's buying in far more materials than we're using at the moment. Fobbed me off with some story about a fixed contract, but I'm sure he was lying.'

'If it's a tax scam he could go to prison. Picture him behind bars next time he has a go at you, but for now just forget about him.'

The sisters bought their favourite food and drink items. It was a family tradition that at least one Christmas present be something unusual bought from the show. Raspberry cream liqueur didn't find its way into either of their shopping bags.

'What next?' Kate asked.

'Lunch. All those tiny nibbles make me more hungry, not less.'

They stopped at the stand of the bank where Kate worked. They were offered crisps and a glass of wine, from a bottle that clearly wasn't chilled. They refused both.

'That was disappointing,' Kate said. 'I was hoping for sandwiches at least.'

'Sandwiches? I don't think so. Hog roast, fresh strawberries and ice cold champagne is what I want.'

'Lovely, if you're paying that is.'

'Not me, Tony.' She produced the notes.

'Even better.'

They followed the delicious scent of roasting pork and joined the queue. If she'd not already been hungry, which would have been a minor miracle, Alice definitely would have been after watching the meat being carved and piled into fresh rolls. When their turn came, both girls said 'yes please' to a dollop each of tangy apple sauce and savoury stuffing as well as a piece of crisp crackling. They'd been right not to buy the wine first, they needed two hands to eat the hog roast rolls without losing half the contents.

Once they had a plastic glass of ice cold champagne each and a large punnet of strawberries between them they found a seat where they could watch the show jumping as they ate and drank. If it hadn't been for the fact they were sitting on straw bales and were dunking the strawberries into sugar from the sachets they'd swiped from one of the fast food stands, Alice would have felt quite sophisticated. At least she had some idea when to clap for a clear round, even if she chose to yell a cheer instead rather than put her glass down and risk spilling the champagne.

When they'd finished, Kate said, 'That was delish. Thank Tony for me, will you?'

Alice didn't bother suggesting Kate do that herself. Whenever the two met at Alice's flat the atmosphere turned so frosty Kate usually phoned first and only visited if he was absent.

'Let's have a look at you,' Kate said. She used her paper serviette to wipe a smear of grease from Alice's chin, made a pretence of fluffing up her hair and said, 'Shoulders back, chest out.'

'Am I about to be inspected or something?'

'It'll be you doing the inspecting. As you know, Hampshire Fire Brigade are located in the next aisle.'

'I don't have some weird sixth sense which enables me to locate firemen.'

'No, but enough interest to memorise the show-ground map.'

'Not difficult as it's generally the same.'

'And we generally pay them a visit. Shall we?'

'I told you...'

'I know, you're over all that stuff. But you still appreciate the valuable service they offer, don't you?'

'Well yes, obviously.'

'And it's tradition that we go see them.'

'OK,' Alice said. 'You've talked me into it.'

Alice noticed one fireman in particular. At around six foot and topped with a mass of curls so sun-bleached they were almost white, he'd have been hard to miss even without the uniform and sexy laugh. Surely it was Handsome Hamish from school? He'd been captain of the sixth form rugby team when she was fourteen and been her first crush. She'd actually had a fantasy that he'd become a fireman and rescue her from a burning building. But then she'd fantasised about her first boyfriend doing that, and her second and Johnny Depp and a man she'd seen on a bus. OK, maybe she did have a thing about firemen. Had. She'd had a thing about firemen but she was absolutely, totally and completely over it.

As the sisters waited their turn, Hamish flirted outrageously with a group of ladies who looked like they'd come to sell jam in the WI marquee. He showed them his big hose and invited them to get a firm grip on it.

'Where's your helmet, young man?' one of them asked.

'Come round the back of the truck and I'll show you.'

Egged on by her friends she went with him and returned wearing it. The helmet was far too big and covered her eyes, so he had to guide her. She seemed to consider that quite an improvement on walking unaided. The women were laughing so much as they walked away they had to use each other for support.

'A couple of hot girls like you obviously need fire safety advice,' Hamish said to Alice and Kate when it was their turn. They were treated to the same sort of silly jokes and dodgy innuendo. After he'd helped them into the firetruck's cab, he said, 'I remember you two, don't I? Applemore School?'

'Correct! I'm Kate and this is my sister Alice. Excuse her if she drools or anything, she has a slight uniform and rubber fetish.'

Alice jabbed her elbow into her traitorous sister's ribs. Normally it would be flattering to be remembered, but she couldn't help wondering exactly what he recalled about her. Had he been aware of quite how often she went to watch rugby practices, or that he was the reason for her interest? Probably not, as she'd been too awestruck to speak to him on the few occasions they'd come face to face, but there was a risk that Kate's comments about drooling would bring it all back.

'Either of you girls like to ring my bell?' Hamish indicated the siren.

'Alice would.' Kate announced a sudden decision to investigate smoke detectors and jumped down from the truck.

'Tactful girl, your sister.'

'I might let her live to regret it.'

'How about coming for a drink with me and we can plot your revenge?' He gave a very attractive grin which made the skin at the sides of his grey-green eyes crinkle.

'I'd love to.'

'Excellent. In the meantime, how do you fancy being rescued from a burning building? The girl who was going to play the part isn't well. You'd just have to wait in a model house while we bring the engine into the main arena and send up the ladder. I'd carry you down in a fireman's lift.'

Alice gaped. He'd just described the first part of her fireman fantasy. The second part started with the kiss of life and didn't require his uniform.

'You'd be perfectly safe, I promise. You might have to borrow some trousers though, that rather nice dress isn't really suitable.'

She was glad Tony didn't hear that. 'Told you so' would be all across his face. Alice sighed. If she were to take part in the display it was bound to get back to Tony who definitely wouldn't be happy. And knowing he wouldn't like it she really shouldn't do it.

'Um I can't. Sorry. Oh...or go for a drink, if you were serious about that. I have a boyfriend.'

He shrugged. 'Of course you have.'

'Sorry. I should... er...'

'It's fine. We'll ask for a volunteer from the audience. Now push that switch there and get that siren going.'

'Will you be going to the school reunion in January?' she asked once she'd climbed down again.

'Hopefully. A lot could happen between now and then. Who knows what might have changed?'

'Might see you there then.'

Hamish was flirting with his next visitors when she and Kate left; a pair of slim, flamboyantly dressed young men who giggled even more than the WI ladies. Perhaps he always acted like that and she'd been mistaken in thinking it was her relationship status he hoped might have changed by January.

'You turned down a fireman?' Kate gasped when Alice told her what she'd missed.

'I know! Mad or what?'

'You must really love Tony.'

'Well...' She still did, didn't she? It didn't mean anything that she wasn't quite able to say so or that a sarcastic little voice in her head was saying, 'Yeah, you absolutely, totally and completely love him.'

## Chapter 2

Alice forced herself to watch the firefighters' display in the main arena. Usually it would have been one of the highlights of the day, but then she hadn't usually been given the chance to be part of it. She'd imagined such a thing before, numerous times, but her thoughts never ended with her turning down the opportunity. Absolutely the opposite.

At first all there was to see was a mock-up of a block of flats, made from a scaffolding framework, clad with board and painted canvas. Soon fake smoke streamed from the top of the building. A blonde leaned out of a window, gesturing frantically to the fire crew below. To Alice she looked more desperate for attention than rescue.

The announcer informed the crowd that the fire brigade were being called and help was on the way. Even before he'd finished, sirens blared and fire engines, blue lights ablaze, rushed to the scene. The fire crews poured from their vehicles and immediately started tackling the flames. They extended a ladder towards the girl's window. A fireman began climbing. Due to the uniform and helmet Alice wouldn't have known it was Hamish unless he'd told her what his role was to be, but in her mind she'd have seen someone just as young, fit and attractive and with a grin just as appealing as his.

'Now there's someone who doesn't get vertigo,' Kate said.

Alice ignored her. She'd long ago given up trying to convince her sister that Tony didn't have a fear of heights. Once Kate got an idea in her head it was almost impossible to shift it.

'Will he reach her in time?' demanded the announcer.

Fake flames, less convincing than the smoke and announcer's pretended doubt over the outcome, leapt in all directions. The firemen on the ground sprayed water. Real water and Alice was pleased to see a little of the spray reached the blonde. If there was any justice her straight locks would be a frizzy mess by the time Hamish got to her. Hopefully her mascara wasn't waterproof.

As the smoke thickened, the girl vanished from sight. The announcer warned of the dangers of smoke inhalation. 'Almost there,' he said as the tall, strong, hunky fireman climbed the last few steps. He too vanished from sight for a moment, then reappeared with the blonde in his arms. It was exactly like Alice's fantasy except for a few little details. In her imagination obviously it would be her getting rescued, her the fireman carried away to safety, her who melted his heart and ignited a fire of passion hotter than any fire he'd faced. Her, not some mystery blonde.

Alice didn't mind about the unconvincing fire, the danger or realities of the situation weren't what appealed to her. She knew her fantasy was just that. Now the blonde girl had ruined it all for Alice. No, it wasn't quite that. Alice had enjoyed similar demonstrations before although she'd not participated in them. It wasn't so much that it wasn't her as the fact she'd said no. That she'd always have to say no.

Hamish climbed down with the girl over his shoulder. The crowd cheered.

'He has her! And it looks like she's grateful.' The announcer stated the obvious as they reached the ground.

Hamish removed his helmet and the blonde hussy attached her, no doubt pouty, lips to the poor chap's mouth.

'That could have been you,' Kate, said.

'Thanks for reminding me,' Alice snapped.

The commentator thanked Hampshire Fire Service for the thrilling demonstration as the sisters left the main arena.

'What do you want to do now?' Kate asked. 'I need the loo, but then we'll do whatever will cheer you up.'

'Can I start the day over?' Alice asked.

'Has it been so bad?'

Had it? She knew she was being silly over the fire display and her disappointment was temporary. Otherwise she'd had a good day, mostly.

'Tony and I rowed this morning over me wearing this.' Alice indicated her dress.

'Bet he only stopped the night so he could remind you not to have any fun today.'

'Don't be like that,' Alice said. 'He has his good points.'

'If you say so. Anyway, I'm glad you didn't cave in.'

'I didn't see why I should. I like this dress.'

'Me too and from the way Handsome Hamish was looking at you, I'm not the only one. I quite understand why you were so keen to wear it today.'

'You sound like Tony!'

'Don't be mean,' Kate said. She joined the queue for the toilets, leaving Alice to sit on a straw bale and wait.

Had she been so wrong to compare Kate with Tony? They both seemed to think the worst of her at times. No, that wasn't fair. Kate had just been teasing and she knew how insecure Tony could be. Maybe she should make more effort not to give him reason to feel like that. It wasn't his fault that he, who spent most of his time working, didn't seem to understand her need to spend time with other people. He'd been very supportive when she'd moved out from her parents' home saying she needed a bit of space. He'd carefully checked her lease agreement, found the best insurance policy for her few items of furniture, most of which he'd paid for, and fitted smoke and carbon monoxide detectors.

He'd understood her satisfaction at her independence, but been confused that she chose to visit her mum and dad several times a week, often sharing a meal. Because Kate still lived there and therefore Alice would see her frequently, it seemed strange to him that the pair of them often went out together in the evenings. He was just as perplexed by her regular meetings with old school friends and former work colleagues, especially as few of Alice's social engagements involved what he referred to as 'culturally enriching experiences'. Tony didn't do fun for the sake of it; why waste time on that when he could be furthering his career, social position or feeling of superiority?

Oh, maybe she did spend slightly too much time with Kate. Surely that last thought was something her sister had put in her head, not one of Alice's own. She quite enjoyed going to exhibitions with Tony and watching plays or the 'right kind' of film. She didn't mind listening to classical music sometimes or being taken to classy places to eat and drink as often as he liked.

The previous week Tony had taken her to a gallery

showcasing the talents of contemporary British artists. Alice knew it was probably a reflection on her poor taste that she didn't totally appreciate the sculptures formed from second-hand chewing gum and text message poetry. They were better than the 'found' music which seemed to be a medley of drills; dentist, pneumatic and the DIY sort. In between was bursts of a man shouting instructions.

'Oh!' she'd said as she deciphered some of the words as 'present arms' and 'eyes front'. 'He's a drill instructor!'

'Who is?' Tony asked. He'd actually seemed impressed by her explanation.

They'd been accosted by a very shiny-faced man dressed entirely in lime green who said the piece was called 'Drilling into Your Soul' and had been written by his partner.

'It's very effective,' Alice said. She'd heard someone say that to the gum sculptor who'd been delighted, so it seemed a safe comment.

'So powerful, isn't it?' the man had said.

Alice and Tony had both agreed that was the case, then moved on to look at paintings of... well she didn't know what they were of, but she did know they represented the futility of progress, because there was a label saying so.

A reflection on her good appetite was her wholehearted appreciation of the snacks. These also had a British theme, but, in order to contrast with the artwork, they were all classics. To begin with cocktail sticks holding bite-sized ploughman's lunches in the form of small chunks of cheddar, apple, celery and pickled onions, some with and some without ham, were offered. Mini Melton Mowbray pork pies, triangles of Welsh rarebit, tiny scotch eggs and bowls of those fancy crisps created from a variety of root vegetables made up the next selection. Once those had all been consumed, trays of teensy lemon meringue pies, treacle tarts and fruit and cream-filled meringues were circulated. The meringues were described as Eton Mess but, although they were composed of the correct ingredients, were far too exquisitely neat to deserve the name. They tasted lovely though, as did the dainty wedges of Stilton, Red Leicester and Cornish Yarg each on different tiny crackers which followed.

Overall Alice had enjoyed that evening. She also liked sitting in a burger place with her mates, wearing whatever she'd happened to have on and laughing at stupid jokes. Or window shopping with Kate, which also generally involved laughing at stupid jokes.

Tony never wasted his time that way, but she couldn't help feeling he was missing out by not having a close family and a bunch of friends he'd never feel he had to impress. It was a good thing he had her and a time consuming job or surely he'd be terribly lonely. Alice didn't want to be without Tony, but she knew she'd have her friends and family for support if they did split up. Loneliness wasn't one of her concerns.

'Sorry I snapped,' Kate said when she returned from the toilets.

'Me too. Come on, I still have some of Tony's money left. Let's get huge ice creams.'

Kate grinned. 'Excellent idea.'


Tony called her that evening to apologise for being grouchy. 'I was annoyed with myself for not going too, but that's no excuse.'

'You missed a good day.' Alice told him about some of the things they'd seen and done, but refrained from mentioning the fire brigade at all. He'd only have read more into it than had actually happened, even though from her point of view that was almost nothing at all. 'Kate says thanks for the lunch,' she added.

'She's very welcome.'

'Oh, and we got the egg on a plate pictures for you.'

'Seriously?'

'Trust me, there's nothing more serious than an egg on a plate to some people. I can tell you all about albumen viscosity if you're interested.'

'Um, well...'

'Don't worry, I can't really remember the details.'

'Then I'll make do with just the pictures.'

The next day he sent a fabulous bouquet of mixed white flowers tied up with a bright pink bow. The exact same pink as her dress. What was he saying? That she'd looked as good as the flowers when she wore it, or was he reminding her that he hadn't forgotten she'd done so against his wishes? The former she decided; she refused to jump to conclusions and think the worst of those she cared about.

The flowers still looked wonderful a week later, which was only the second time she'd seen Tony since the New Forest Show. On Sunday, they'd gone to an exhibition of more paintings which didn't seem to actually be of anything in particular.

'They express youth, vitality and urgency,' Tony had

explained.

'Yes, I can see that,' Alice agreed. Well, to her they looked as though five-year-olds had done them. Five-year-olds in a hurry, so that was sort of the same thing.

'Do you like them?'

'I prefer them to those futility ones we saw,' she said. That was quite true, but then she'd rather have a filling than root canal surgery.

'Do you have a favourite?'

Alice pointed to the nicest coloured one of those which already had red 'sold' stickers on it, secure in the knowledge that someone else valued it and Tony wouldn't be able to buy it as either a gift or an investment. It was the sort of thing he might well do. Chocolates or Premium Bonds respectively would make much more sense to her.

Afterwards they'd gone out for a meal. The food was delicious and presented in such an artistic way that it more than made up for the paintings seeming a bit messy. They were joined by two acquaintances of Tony's. The men were very serious and spoke about the grown-up subjects of corporate insurance and carbon trade exchange in such detail they made up for any childishness, not just in the artwork but in the world ever. Still, Tony seemed interested, so she smiled and nodded, particularly when the waiter suggested another bottle of Chablis.

Since then Tony had been too busy with work to go out socially. He'd phoned several times though. He always called her if he knew she'd gone out. That was because he cared about her and wanted to know she'd got home safely. It was not, as Kate insinuated, because he was checking up on her.

A week later, Alice had a surprise as she finished work. Tony was waiting outside.

'I realised I've been neglecting you lately,' he said as he opened his car door for her.

'I know you've been busy with work,' Alice said, trying hard to sound sympathetically understanding rather than neglected. 'Have you finished the latest project?'

'We have, so I'll be back to normal hours for a while now.'

Alice almost asked, 'Normal for you, or actually normal?' but stopped herself just in time.

'So, where shall we go?'

'My place, Kate's coming to tea.'

'Ah. Lovely.

When Kate arrived she showed him the photos she'd taken at the show. 'There you go, eggs on plates.'

Tony studied the images. 'No doubt about it, those are eggs on plates.'

'Surely you didn't doubt something Alice told you?' Kate asked.

'Of course not. There's no reason for me to is there?'

'Show him the Highland cows,' Alice said. 'The calves are so cute, Tony. Look at that gingery one, he was my favourite.'

Tony looked at the picture of Alice cuddling the animal, her arms lost in its deep fur, and its huge tongue attempting to lick her hair. 'So I see!'

'And there's his mum.'

'You're very close. Are you sure it was safe?'

'Deffo. They're gentle and anyway, they're tied up.'

'OK.'

Alice knew that if he'd gone to the cattle lines at all, he'd have picked his way through the straw on the ground, keeping as far away from the animals as possible.

Tony smiled tolerantly at the images of Alice on a helter-skelter and eating candyfloss. 'You seem to have acted like big kids,' was his opinion.

'That's part of the fun,' Alice said. Maybe it was as well he hadn't come with them, it wasn't really his sort of thing.

'You know what fun is, Tony?' Kate said. 'It's that thing other people have when you're not about.'

'Yes, I know what it is and I'm glad Alice has her charming sister to help her indulge whilst I'm busy.'

Kate showed him a picture of Alice in the fire engine. 'The firemen were happy to help too.' She didn't even try not to smirk.

'Anyone want a drink?' Alice asked brightly. If she acted like they were all getting along, maybe it'd come true.

It didn't work. Kate soon left and Tony continued to sulk. She knew he loved her, but wished he'd show it in a way which didn't involve jealousy or buying her things.

'Have you thought any more about moving in with me?' he asked, proving she should be careful what she wished for.

She had, mostly trying to figure out why she was so reluctant. Tony's flat was plenty big enough for them both and he'd promised to have it redecorated to suit her.

Tony had lots of good points. He was generous. He cared

about her safety, insisting on paying for taxis whenever she went anywhere without him. He'd wanted her to take one to work when he realised how far off the road, and therefore the bus route, the premises were. Her parents liked him. They'd suggested she not rush into anything though.

'My contract for this place has another six months to run. Maybe after that?' Alice suggested.

'You'll have to decide before then and let them know if you're not going to renew the lease.'

She was aware of that but determined not to be pushed into a decision she wasn't ready for.

'I'll give you an answer by the new year, OK? Please don't ask again until then.'

'New year! But that's months away.' He must have seen her expression because he raised his hands in surrender. 'All right. If you make up your mind before then just say and I'll book the decorators, but I promise not to ask again before that.'

Alice considered fetching the pink ribbon from her flowers and saying as they both liked the colour so much they should have the walls all done to match, but decided it might be sending the wrong signals. If they started looking at paint colour charts she'd find herself swept along with his plans. That happened all too often as it was.

'By the way,' he said, 'I'm not working late Friday night after all, so I've booked us a table at Luigi's.'

Alice took a deep breath. Luigi's served the absolute best Florentine pizza, lushest creamiest tiramisu and the bubbliest prosecco in the prettiest crystal glasses... 'Sorry, I can't.'

'I thought it was your favourite restaurant.'

'It is and I'd love to go another time, but I've promised to go to Mum and Dad's. Dad is putting up a new shed and Kate and I are supervising.'

'In the dark?'

'Dad'll put the security light on. It's really bright.'

'Oh. OK. You'll still have to eat. We can go afterwards.'

'Afterwards we'll be getting fish and chips from the van which comes round. You know we always do that after one of Dad's projects.'

'Oh.' He should do, they'd had fish and chips waiting for him when he got out the shower the time he'd helped repair the fence. How he'd ended up in the pond on that occasion and therefore needed a shower was a mystery. Even Kate, who'd been very nearby, said she didn't have a clue. He'd not been available during any of her dad's projects since, but she'd told him about them.

'You can come with me if you like. I'm sure it'd help to have someone tall on top of the ladder.' That wasn't fair and she knew it. DIY was most definitely not his kind of thing, especially when it happened out of doors.

'Right, OK.'

'Tony, you don't have to. Kate's rounded up a few of the chaps she works with, so I'm sure they'll be enough people to get it done.'

'No really, I'd like to help and I haven't seen your parents lately.'

Tony borrowed a pair of old jeans from Alice's dad, so as not to get his chinos dirty. He wore gloves to avoid splinters, protective goggles to stop roofing tacks injuring his eyes, and kept a good distance from Kate for no specified reason. Although he looked a bit daft, he did a good job of reading the instructions so tasks weren't attempted until all the right parts and equipment were to hand and were done in the correct order so no time was wasted.

He didn't actually manhandle any pieces of the shed, but he did pick up a claw hammer at one point. That's because one of Kate's friends asked him to pass it up.

'Sure. Er, a claw hammer...?'

'In the bucket by your feet. The thing with the orange handle.'

Tony also double-checked the measurements before Alice's dad cut the roofing felt. Both figures matched, but he didn't take offence.

'It's good to be sure about things,' he said. 'Better than rushing in without thinking things through.'

'That seems to be a family trait,' Tony said. Then after an awkward pause added, 'And an admirable one too.'

Alice guessed he was referring to her indecision about moving in with him, but he kept his promise of not asking again and didn't mention it, at least not outright. He must have been tempted though when her dad thanked him for his help and offered to return the favour, 'If you ever have anything wanting doing at your place.'

Instead he waited until her mum asked if everyone wanted fish for supper, or if Tony would rather have a sausage in batter.

'To be honest, I've got a real fancy for pizza. How about I get us all a take-away from Luigi's, my treat?' he said.

Alice decided it wouldn't hurt to let him have his own way this once and the others, including Kate, were clearly in favour too.

'Thanks, lad,' Alice's dad said. 'While you're doing that I'll open up some of the beetroot wine I made last summer. Should be maturing nicely now.'

'That sounds nice, but unfortunately I'm driving,' Tony said, just before Alice could utter the same sentence.

'Oh what a shame,' Kate said. 'Let me know when you're coming next and I'll pick you up so you can have lots.'

'So kind, but I'd really hate you to miss out on a single drop.'

Alice hastily asked everyone what they wanted to eat before her dad realised they were all more keen to ensure other people got to sample his wine than they were to drink it themselves. He was so proud of making it and so not wasting any of the fruit and vegetables he grew and really it didn't taste too bad if you added enough lemonade.

Tony frequently encouraged Alice to stay with him and suggested cooking meals for her parents would be easier in his large kitchen than with her two gas rings and tiny grill. That was very true and as he even made an effort to make Kate welcome, Alice spent quite a lot of time playing house at his place.

One afternoon Tony took her to get supplies for Sunday roast for the five of them.

'I need to phone Rachel, I'll meet you back here in an hour,' he said.

Alice rushed round the supermarket so as not to keep him waiting. She was outside and out of breath, with a pile of bags at her feet, forty minutes later.

'Alice?'

She turned to see Hamish. She felt her heart bump in a way she knew it wouldn't have if it had been Tony saying her name.

## Chapter 3

'Can I offer you a lift?' Hamish asked.

'Thanks but I'm being picked up... by my boyfriend.'

'Ah well, can't win them all.'

'No.' She thought of the supermarket carrier bags at her feet and the message they might be sending. Unaccountably it seemed important that Hamish didn't think her relationship with Tony was more serious than was actually the case. 'I'm cooking Sunday lunch at his place for a few people.'

'Lucky them, I seem to remember you're a good cook.'

'You do?' One term her home economics teacher had the bright idea of allowing pupils to cook for staff, family members or friends who would come and share the food in the lunch break. Alice had teamed up with another girl who was going out with a member of the rugby team and they'd arranged that her boyfriend come and bring Hamish. Alice didn't say a word. That was partly because her friend Melanie was a chatterbox and partly because being so close to Hamish their knees occasionally touched under the table, had made it hard for her to breathe normally.

'Yep. Well sort of. To be honest your friend's cooking made more of an impression. It went badly wrong, didn't it?'

'Oh, that's right! Melanie accidentally put mint flavouring in her lemon drizzle and it tasted really strange.'

'It looked a bit odd too.'

'Yeah.'

'And was weirdly crunchy.'

'She wasn't good at cracking eggs.' Nor weighing ingredients, or reading labels or instructions actually, but Hamish had probably worked that out at the time. 'Maybe just as well she didn't do cooking as a GCSE subject.'

'Did you?'

'Um hmm. Got an A.' Her one and only.

They continued to talk about school until Alice remembered Tony would be back soon. She glanced at her watch; he wasn't due for ten minutes.

'I'd better get on,' Hamish said. 'See you around.'

Tony pulled up just as he was walking away. 'Who was that?'

'Just someone asking where the nearest cash point is.' She knew she was in the wrong for lying to him and that there was a problem with their relationship if she felt she must do that to prevent a row. She also felt bad that Hamish might have thought she was bored talking to him and looked at her watch as a hint for him to go. He was a nice, friendly man and she didn't want him thinking she was rude.

'Get everything you needed?' Tony asked.

'I did. And I took your advice about not making too much work for myself. We're having strawberries and cream for dessert. You can't get easier than that.' Although what her dad would have to say about buying the fruits out of season was another matter.

'Sounds good. We could have a glass of Premier Cotes de Bordeaux with them.'

'That's the really sweet one Mum likes isn't it?'

'It is. To go with the beef, I thought the Shiraz your sister is fond of.'

'Good idea.' She didn't mention that, unless their dad had made it, Kate couldn't tell one red wine from another and had only been so enthusiastic about the Shiraz because she'd drunk three large glasses of the stuff.

Tony carried in the shopping and asked what he could do to help.

'Lay the table, you get it so much neater than I do.'

He did that, decanted the red wine and made an attempt at peeling the potatoes. Every time she saw him in the kitchen she realised how sensible it was for him to eat out most of the time.

'Actually, could you hull the strawberries?' He could do that without a knife. Alice made a mental note never to let Kate witness Tony at work in a kitchen. She'd be bound to make a crack about the need to keep him away from sharp objects.

The others arrived so precisely on time Alice guessed they'd arrived early and waited round the corner.

'Didn't know what we were having, so I've brought red and white,' her dad said, handing Tony two bottles.

He studied the labels carefully. 'Carrot and dandelion, and elderberry and radish. They sound flavourful combinations.'

'Oh they are. Actually maybe a bit too much with the white one. Think I'll just use dandelion flowers next time, not the leaves as well.'

'Er, yes. Is it quite dry?'

'I suppose you could say that. Got a bit of a kick to it.'

'Right. Not a dessert wine then and we're having beef, so I

think we'd better save the white for another time.'

Seeing half the battle was won, Alice reminded Tony that he'd bought Kate's favourite Shiraz specially. 'You know, Kate, the one you had on my birthday and really liked.'

'Oh yes! Lovely wine that was. I mean yours is too, Dad obviously, but if Tony got that specially then perhaps...?'

'That's settled then,' Tony said. 'I'm keeping hold of these though. I'll save them for exactly the right occasion.' He raised the bottles as though they were trophies, leaving Alice to wonder if he was expecting imminent trouble with the drains.

Kate and her mum both gave him grateful smiles. If he'd returned them to Alice's dad they knew who'd have to drink them. Her dad only ever had a few sips of alcohol, just in case he had to drive anywhere. It was a habit he'd acquired when he'd been on call out and had never broken.

'You know, Tony's not all bad,' Kate said, after she'd played an active part in getting through the first course and two bottles of red and was helping to carry the used crockery back to the kitchen.

'He has lots of good points.'

'Yes, so you keep saying. You must have nearly convinced yourself it's true by now.'

'What do you mean by that?'

'Nothing, Sis. Oh come on, let's not argue. If he's the one for you I'm sure I'll learn to like him eventually. Shall I put these in the dishwasher?'

'No, Tony will do it. He has a system.'

'Yet another of his good points.'

'Yes actually; it means I never have to do it as somehow I always get something in the wrong place.'

'Clever of you.'


Kate called Alice at work on a particularly foul day in early November. 'If you don't have anything else planned I'll pick you up from work tonight, save you getting the bus.'

'That'd be great. Tony's taking me out for a meal tonight, but not until about eight, so we've time for tea and a chat first.'

'Where are you going?'

'Luigi's.'

'Lucky thing.'

'Even though I'll be with Tony?'

'Of course! I know we sometimes rub each other up the wrong way, but he's not so bad really and I have to admit he's generous.'

Alice saw her friend Kath pull a strange face and set about her keyboard with a lot more energy than was generally the case.

'I'm glad to have been able to help. Thank you for using Tatisuz.' Alice hung up on her sister and gave her boss, Miles Molde, her most charming smile. 'Did you want me for something?'

'Yes, there are some letters I want you to send.'

The rest of the afternoon was a combination of taking dictation and writing letters to disgruntled customers, trying to convince them that they'd not really been fobbed off with inferior goods, but had in fact been supplied with items far superior to those which they'd ordered.

'What's wrong with these people?' Miles had asked at one point. Guessing that was possibly a rhetorical question, but if it wasn't he wouldn't welcome her pointing out that not a single customer had contacted them with thanks for a better product and therefore it was his shoddy merchandise which was the problem, she'd kept quiet. Five thirty seemed a long time coming, but she finally made her escape into the warmth of Kate's car and company.

'Have you heard that thing about the differences in your ring sizes predicting your health?' Kate asked on the drive to Alice's flat.

'No, how do you mean?'

'If the, er middle finger and thumb are bigger than the others, then you'll have good health into old age, but if not then you've probably got, um high blood pressure or some other things. You know, stuff that needs looking at, or something.'

Alice glanced at her own hands, then at Kate's on the steering wheel. 'Surely everyone's middle finger and thumb are bigger than their other fingers?'

'Apparently not. We'll try it when we get in, shall we?'

'OK, if you like.' Something was up with Kate. First her being relatively nice about Tony and now this mumbo jumbo. Was she worried about her health or had a row with her boyfriend? Alice hoped not, obviously she didn't want her sister to be sick and she liked Pete who seemed a good match for Kate. Maybe someone had said she had fat fingers? If that was the problem Alice knew what to suggest; that Kate wear tight jeans then all the attention would be on her big bum! She'd have to make sure her escape route was clear before offering that piece of advice though.

Once they had mugs of tea and a plate of biscuits, Kate produced a ring gauge which she insisted Alice try on each finger of both hands. She wrote down each of the sizes.

'So, how's my blood pressure?' Alice asked once she'd finished.

'All right I should think, why?'

'The ring sizes?'

'Oh, er, yes. Like I said you're fine if your thumb is biggest.'

'This whole thing is complete rubbish, isn't it?'

Kate slowly ate a biscuit. 'Yeah, OK it is.'

'So what's up?'

'Nothing.'

'Don't give me that.'

'Nothing, honestly.'

'Are you worried about your health?'

Kate shook her head.

'Or Mum and Dad?'

'No. Well, obviously they're a constant worry, but it's nothing new. Did I tell you Dad has decided to have a go at making Brussels sprout champagne to go with our Christmas dinner?'

'No! We'll have... Don't change the subject. Is everything OK with Pete?'

'Fine. He can't afford to take me to Luigi's every week, but then not many people could.'

'That's because not many people work late most days and part of every weekend practically.'

'Guess not. Tony really is working though, isn't he? The man seems to be obsessed with his job, so I'm sure it's just that.'

Alice nodded. Hmm, Kate sticking up for Tony. What was going on? 'What is going on, Kate?'

'Nothing.'

'You just randomly wanted to know my ring sizes for no particular reason?'

'Look, just don't ask me, OK? You know I'm no good at this stuff and I can't keep a secret.'

'All right, as long as there really isn't anything wrong?' Alice asked.

'Not at all. Quite the opposite in fact.' She said that convincingly.

'And you were kidding about the sprout champagne, weren't you?'

'Sorry, no.'

'We have to stop him.'

'Obviously. But how?'

'Don't rush me, I'm thinking.'

'I'll make more tea, don't want to dehydrate while I wait.'

Alice gave her a look.

'Because this is a difficult problem and genius takes time is what I meant!'

While Kate was in the kitchen, Alice tried to push away memories of the last time her dad had tried making sparkling wine. Three bottles had exploded which had been a tragedy, but only because he'd made nine.

'How many sprouts is he growing, do you know?' she called.

'Not that many, I don't think.' Kate returned carrying mugs. 'This time he's not trying to use up a surplus, he actually thinks it will be a good idea.'

'Maybe we can convince him it will be more special if there's just the one bottle? Between us we should be able to get through that. We could say we're saving the best to last and have it when we're past caring.'

'Could work. The uncles will bring a bottle or three and you said Tony was going to bring wine. Can you persuade him to go for quantity rather than quality just the once? It's not that I mind having my palette educated, but once it has been, Dad's stuff will seem even worse.'

'I've got it! We tell him that Tony's selected a special wine for the toast.'

'Which he probably has,' Kate said. She didn't even sound sneering about it.

'Probably, so it'll be believable. And then we say he and the uncles will be terribly hurt if we don't drink what they've provided.'

'True again. Anyone would be hurt drinking Dad's sprout surprise I should think. Do you want me to have a quiet word and say it'd be better to enjoy the sprouts as a vegetable?'

'No, I'll do it. You're no good at these sorts of things, are you?' Alice said.

'True enough. I'll leave it with you then and I'll leave you to get ready for your evening out. Have fun at Luigi's.'

As Alice showered and then blow-dried her hair the point of that ring size business began to make sense. Clearly someone must want to know what size ring would fit her. And they'd only want to know that if they were planning on giving her a ring. And Kate had said several nice things about Tony and even seemed quite pleased he was joining them for Christmas dinner... or at any rate, was doing her best to seem positive about him. He must be going to propose and had asked Kate to find out what size engagement ring to buy!

A romantic proposal was one of Alice's fantasies. Not the main one, but it was quite high up. In her fantasies the man doing the proposing had usually just featured in her major fantasy by rescuing her from a burning building, at great personal risk, as his life meant nothing without her. Tony was never going to live up to that; maybe no man ever would. That was silly schoolgirl stuff though. A perfectly normal proposal would be just as wonderful if the right man were doing the asking and she was ready to say yes.

Alice still hadn't absolutely decided about moving in with Tony. Living on her own was still a novelty and she wasn't yet ready to give it up. She probably would move in with him fairly soon and she might well marry him eventually, but not yet. No romantic proposal should get the response, 'Can I think about it for a year or two and get back to you?' She had to stop him asking until she was ready to squeal 'yes' and cover his face in ecstatic kisses.

As usual, Tony was greeted warmly, in Italian, at Luigi's. Tony responded enthusiastically. One evening a week was taken up with a 'languages for business' course and he practised whenever he could. On this occasion he ordered their meal faultlessly, at least that's what the waiter said. Alice did recognise a few food names but for the most part Tony could have been talking about his stamp collection and she'd have been none the wiser. Thank goodness he didn't really do that. Listening to him speak Italian was a lot sexier than looking at second-hand stamps. Actually listening to him speak Italian was quite sexy without comparing it with anything.

'Can you say something to me in Italian?' she asked.

'*Sei bello. Mi piaci. Ti amo, bella*, Alice.'

'That sounds nice. Oh, *grazie*, that's what I should say, isn't it?'

'Yes, and then I'd say *prego*.'

Eh? Was he saying he wanted to get her pregnant? No. She was positive he didn't want children yet and even if he did, he'd have a sensible conversation about it not drop an easily misunderstood hint. 'I think something has got lost in translation.'

'I was saying, as far as my vocabulary allows, that you are beautiful and that I like you a great deal. I love you.'

'*Grazie*. I *amore* you *duo*... that wasn't right, was it?'

'Not quite, but I get the idea.' His smile was close to a grin.

The waiter brought their wine, which he opened and poured with just the right amount of ceremony.

'*Grazie*,' Alice said.

'*Prego, Signorina.*'

'Ah! *Prego* means you are welcome.' Maybe if she ate enough pizza she'd eventually learn to speak whole sentences?

When they were sipping sparkling wine in the candlelight, Tony began to fidget. He looked unsettled and reached into his jacket pocket. Oh help! Was he getting ready to propose now? She reached across and took his free hand.

'Tony, can I say something?'

'Yes of course, but can it wait a minute? My phone keeps ringing, well it's set to silent obviously but it's vibrating. It might be important. Do you mind if I take it?'

'Oh, no. Carry on.' He didn't make a habit of chatting to other people on the phone when he was with her, in fact he considered such behaviour rude, so it probably was important. That explained why he'd seemed uncomfortable too. Of course he wasn't going to propose there and then. If he'd asked Alice to secretly find out her ring size, then he'd wait until he'd bought the ring. All she had to do now was persuade him not to do that just yet.

Tony was back in a few minutes. 'I'm sorry about that. I was right though, it was important. We've just landed a huge new contract with a Chinese company.'

'Oh, great news.'

'It is. We've been working towards this for some time and it means... but never mind that, you wanted to say something?'

'Oh, yes. Well, it's just um... Well I know you love me and

want to be with me and I do love you, it's...'

'You've made a decision about moving in with me? You don't want to?'

'No it's not that. Well, not exactly. I'm still thinking. Oh dear, this is difficult.'

'It's OK, Alice. You can tell me.' He took her hands in his.

How on earth do you tactfully suggest to someone, who you've just said you love, not to ask you to marry them? 'Oh dear, I'm no better at this sort of thing than Kate is.'

'Kate? What does she have to do with this?'

'She was asking about my ring sizes.'

'Oh.' He took a sip of wine. 'Oh! You're not sure about living with me as my girlfriend, but maybe another arrangement would suit you better?' He took another drink from his wine glass, more like a gulp than a sip, rose from his seat, walked round to her side of the table and began to sink down onto one knee.

## Chapter 4

Alice grabbed Tony's hand and attempted to pull him to his feet. 'No, Tony, please don't.'

He rose, kissed her cheek and returned to his own seat. He looked confused, but not horribly disappointed. Actually, if her sense of pride would have allowed it, she'd have thought he looked almost relieved.

'Sorry, I said I wasn't very good at this...' Alice mumbled. 'I got a silly idea into my head, but honestly I wasn't trying to push you into something you're not ready for.'

'No, I see that.'

'And you're not ready, are you? For um...' she gestured to where he'd been about to kneel. 'Excuse me a minute.' Alice made a dash for the toilets and took several deep breaths. What should she do now? She was tempted to just leave via the fire exit, but that would be cowardly and horribly unfair to Tony.

What then, pretend that had never happened? It was still a cop out, but probably her best choice. Alice vowed never again to wish Tony would do something spontaneously romantic.

She studied her unchanged face in the mirror, applied an unnecessary coat of lipstick and returned. Tony was still there, looking only a little more awkward than you'd expect from a man whose date has abruptly left him sitting on his own.

He smiled as she took her seat opposite. This time there

was real relief on his face. Thank goodness she'd not given into her impulse to run away.

The waiter brought their antipasti just then, so they were both able to concentrate on the food. After a few comments about the tang of the tapenade and the succulence of the olives, Alice asked about the new contract.

'Will you get to go to China, do you think?'

'It's unlikely, but if the opportunity arose I'd certainly take it.'

'How about learning Chinese?'

Tony spoke a few words which she didn't understand.

'Seriously? That was Chinese?'

'I can only manage a few phrases of Mandarin. I just said, 'hello, nice to meet you' and 'thank you'. That's about my limit and I'm pretty sure people only understand what I'm saying because it's what they expect to hear.'

'Well, I'm impressed.'

'The people I've dealt with seem pleased I make the effort, even though they all speak excellent English.'

'I suppose it's polite if you can do it. You'll have to teach Rachel.'

Tony shook his head. 'She's much better than me. The absolute star pupil on our course.'

'Oh.' It hadn't occurred to Alice that Rachel would be taking the same course too, but perhaps it should have. She and Tony worked so closely together that naturally they'd need the same kind of skills. All the same she couldn't help wondering what his reaction would have been if she'd casually dropped into the conversation that she spent one evening a week with an attractive male work colleague whom she greatly admired. Mentally she ran through the Tatisuz staff. She quite admired Kath. Lucy and Emma were both pretty. Miles and most of the warehouse staff were male, but there wasn't anyone who matched up to all three categories.

'Alice, about Christmas...'

'Don't tell me you've got to work over Christmas.'

'No of course not. Why would you think that?'

Because he'd sounded unsure of himself which wasn't usual and because he'd been unable to accompany her to previous family events because of work. He'd never actually let her down though, not when it really mattered and had already been arranged.

'So you're coming?' she asked.

'Of course, that's if you and your parents want me to.'

'Of course they do. Kate too actually.'

'Is there some particular reason for that?'

She couldn't blame him for sounding dubious. 'Dad's planning to serve Brussels sprout wine.'

'He has to be stopped!'

'Exactly what I said and we have a plan.' She explained the idea she and Kate had, for him to supply some bubbly. 'It doesn't have to be expensive stuff, anything which actually comes from grapes would be good.'

'Don't worry, I'm sure I can find a few suitable bottles.'

Alice had no doubts whatsoever about that.

'So what is it about Christmas?'

'The gifts. What should I give your family?' Tony asked.

'The same sort of things as last year would be perfect.' She'd explained the previous year that they always gave each other several small gifts, rather than big, expensive presents. She'd left out the part about them often coming from the New Forest Show because he hadn't gone. As that was still the case, she still didn't mention it. Tony's offerings of gourmet chocolates, hand-made (but not by him) shortbread and glass bowls filled with whole candied fruits had been well received.

They'd each been identically and professionally wrapped, presumably in the shop where he bought them, but no one had seemed inclined to hold that against him. Kate did say she hoped the ones they'd sent him wouldn't clash with his tree decorations and give him a migraine, but as she'd used a pink patterned wrap and a glow in the dark yellow bow for his musical socks, maybe she'd been expressing genuine remorse.

'Is that all?' Tony asked.

'Yes, definitely.' He didn't seem to realise that giving up the quiet elegant day he'd otherwise have enjoyed so that Alice could spend a chaotic few hours with both her family and her boyfriend was actually the important bit.

'All right, if that's what you think is best. But what about you? Am I allowed to buy you a proper, useful gift?'

Proper and useful weren't words Alice associated with Christmas presents, but if he really wanted to buy her something expensive then it might as well be something she'd like.

'Well my hair straighteners are past their best and my

laptop is running really slowly.' It didn't help that Kate kept borrowing the straighteners and Alice had to use the computer for work as her boss still hadn't replaced the ancient desktops in the office.

'I'll get you a laptop then.'

'Thank you.' Why did he have to tell her? Guessing what the gift could be was one of the things she enjoyed about Christmas.


Works parties were one of the Christmas traditions she could do without. She'd thought there wasn't going to be one for Tatisuz that year as Miles said he couldn't afford it.

'I've already given you extra days off over Christmas,' he said. It was true he'd said they needn't go in at all from the day before Christmas Eve until the first working day in the new year, if they all gave up just one day of their holiday entitlement. They all knew that was because he wanted the time off himself and there was never anything for them to do then anyway as their customers didn't place orders over the festive period. He'd save money on heating too, which was probably the main reason for his pretended generosity.

'It needn't cost anything, Mr Scrooge,' Kath had told him. 'Just let us use the warehouse. It'll be pretty empty by then, won't it?'

'Not the way things are going,' Miles said.

'There'll be space; it's half empty now. We can bring our own food and drink.'

'Oh, go on boss, it'll be fun,' Emma added. She hadn't been there the previous year so could be excused not knowing that it wouldn't really be much fun. What there didn't seem to be any excuse for was the way she was batting those enormous eyelashes at Miles. She'd definitely been there long enough to know what a slime-ball he was.

'Oh all right. And you can pick up some crisps and mince pies at the cash and carry, Kath, to make sure there really is some food.'

Aha! So Emma did know what she was doing after all.

She'd given Tony the 'good' news that evening. 'I'll have to go I suppose. You don't have to though.'

'Why do you want to go on your own?'

'I don't particularly want to go at all, Tony. It'll be OK, but no better than an extended lunch break with added booze and far more opportunity for the warehouse boys to make inappropriate comments.'

'Then it sounds as though you'll need me.'

Seriously? He really thought she could be the slightest bit interested in any of that lot? Well, for once she wouldn't be the one to suffer from his jealousy. Knowing that the more she protested the greater would be his determination she said, 'It really won't be your sort of thing at all and don't worry, I can handle that lot and I'll have Kath for back-up.'

'Even so, I'd like to come.'

'Brilliant! I'll drive then, so you can have fun.' No need to tell him about the bring a bottle part, or that her contribution would be a crate of her dad's nettle beer. Nor that she'd be putting his name down for the karaoke.

Alice felt mean about her actions by the time the staff of Tatisuz decided on a date for the party and that it would be fancy dress. It was the same date as Tony's own work's do.

Having said he'd come to hers and seeing her looked pleased about it, he wouldn't back out. She didn't mind him wasting a few dull hours realising he had no reason to be concerned about her falling for the charms of her colleagues. She didn't mind him having the embarrassment of singing in public and having to do it completely sober because there'd be nothing drinkable on offer. It didn't seem fair though that because of it he'd miss out on an event which he'd actually enjoy. Didn't seem fair because it wasn't.

'How about we go to yours? We could drop off Dad's beer and say hello at mine first so we don't seem unsociable, but it'll get us out of the fancy dress and the karaoke.'

Tony blinked. She guessed that someone taken from the Tower of London into the sunlight and realising they were being freed rather than having their head placed on the block might blink in much the same way.

'I did say I didn't think it would be your sort of thing,' she reminded him. Tony's own work party wasn't likely to be Alice's sort of thing, but she kept that to herself.

He quickly agreed with her suggestion.

Tony told her the event hosted by his employer would be quite formal and the partners' wives often wore full evening dresses. He did so tactfully, with no veiled hints that her usual dress code wouldn't do, so she wanted to wear something which would please him. The dress she chose was floor length, in silvery grey silk. It left her shoulders bare but wasn't low cut enough to startle anyone. She'd expected Kate to say it was too prim and proper, but her sister didn't take that view.

'It's classy, but sexy too. Normally it'd be a shame to cover up your assets, but when you're covering them with silk so soft you want to stroke it, that's a different matter.'

'You think Tony will approve?'

'Bet you a chocolate éclair you either have to throw a bucket of cold water over him, or get to the party late.'

Alice wore half her usual amount of make-up and far more jewellery than she was used to. That too was classy stuff, lent to her by Tony's mother. Although it all made her feel a little as though she was in fancy dress after all, Tony clearly approved as much as Kate thought he would. So much so that Alice thought they might not make it to either party.

'You're gorgeous and I'm so proud of you,' he said as his hands moved over the slinky fabric and he pulled her close against him.

'So I see! Don't wrinkle me though, I haven't a clue how to get creases out of this.'

'Then I'll take it off very carefully.'

'Yes, but later. Much later.'

He groaned but she wriggled free and stuck the crate of beer in his arms. 'Keep a good hold of that, you won't want it exploding in your car.'

'Is that likely?'

'Not with this batch, it's gone a bit flat apparently.'

'But you're still taking it. Do you actually hate your work colleagues?'

'Someone has to drink the stuff... If you can make sure Miles is one of those people I'll be verrrry grateful.' She floated a hand along the neckline of her dress as she spoke.

He managed it too. Alice smiled as she watched Miles take a big gulp of slightly warm, slightly flat and totally disgusting nettle beer. Just as he looked as though he would gag, Tony told him Alice had supplied the drink and it was her Christmas gift to her boss and the forklift truck drivers. None of them could avoid consuming a whole bottle of the stuff each after that.

Tony wasn't tempted by the plates of scotch eggs, pork pies cut into wedges and bowls of suspiciously orange crisps. Alice could see his point, but she'd need to eat something during the evening.

'Will there be food at yours?' she asked Tony.

'Oh yes, they always serve a good selection of canapés.'

That didn't sound very substantial to Alice so she had a scotch egg. It was OK once she'd dipped it in brown sauce.

In less than an hour Alice was driving them to Tony's flat. They left the car there and got a taxi to the gallery where his office party was being held.

She'd have found it hard to chat animatedly about hedge funds, aggregated limits of indemnity and liquidity ratios even if she'd been totally sure what they all meant. When asked about her golf handicap she had to admit it was not having a clue where her nearest course could be found.

Clients had also been invited to the event, including several Chinese, so Tony's attention and even presence were often diverted from her. The only other person Alice knew at all was Rachel. She did come over and speak when she saw Alice on her own, but she too was busy with clients. As a networking opportunity no doubt it was very useful, but it wasn't what Alice called a party.

On the plus side, the food and drink were superb and plentiful. Every few minutes Alice was presented with silver platters of tempting items. Miniature Yorkshire puddings filled with a sliver of tender beef and decorated with a delicate swirl of mustard and a single brilliant green pea looked fabulous and tasted even better. They were still warm and the batter as crisp as though her mum had just taken it out the oven. There were delicate little walnut biscuits, rich onion tartlets no bigger than a 50p piece and olives stuffed with cream cheese and decorated with red pepper so they looked like the cutest little penguins. Alice just had to get a picture of those. Guessing photographing their food wasn't something the other guests would do, Alice loitered in a corridor on the way back from the ladies room and waylaid a waitress.

Alice was tempted by the trays of cocktails too, but she'd accepted a glass of champagne when she arrived and thought it better not to mix her drinks. The music came from an actual piano played by an actual pianist and Alice at least looked as though she fitted in.

Tony returned to her side. 'Sorry, I didn't mean to be gone so long. Shall I take you round now and introduce you to a few people?'

'It's OK, I'm fine sat here listening to the music if you need to go schmooze.'

'If you're sure?'

'Definitely.'

'Thank you. I will take you round and show you off soon though, then I'm going to take you home and get you out that dress before it can even think of wrinkling.' He kissed her cheek and headed back into the crowd.

'Can I offer you a drink, madam?' enquired an immaculate waiter.

'Thank you.' Alice accepted another glass of perfectly chilled champagne and another quail's egg wrapped in a delicious savoury coating.

Perhaps Christmas parties weren't so bad after all.


Christmas Day was the usual sort of chaos. Alice's uncles came. She had four. Two were real ones, her dad's bother Mark and her mum's brother Nigel. The other two were always referred to as uncles, but were actually a cousin of some kind and his partner. Confusingly they were called Pete and Peter, which was also the name of Alice's dad. They were Kate and Alice's unofficial godfathers, sending random gifts now and then from around the world and coming for Christmas lunch those years they were in the country. Another guest was Petra, an elderly neighbour who seemed to have no family. She always arrived after the morning church service, said grace as the turkey was carved, and left in time to attend evensong. Along with Tony, Alice's boyfriend, who was another Pete, and Mark's wife Jan, that meant twelve people to feed.

'Alice,' Tony whispered. 'I didn't realise there would be so many people, I haven't brought nearly enough wine.'

'Yes you have, it's just for the toast. There's plenty of other stuff.' She knew there was, she'd seen it chilling in buckets in the garage. Tony didn't seem convinced.

'Other stuff which Dad didn't make, I mean.'

'OK, but I still wish I'd known. I'd have bought more.'

That's why she hadn't told him. The champagne he'd brought had a year printed on the label, not the name of a supermarket. She couldn't even guess what it cost.

Alice's dad made a toast and everyone, Petra included, enjoyed the champagne.

'Just as your father turns vegetables into wine, the Lord did with water,' she said when Kate offered her a glass.

'It's not quite the same I don't think,' Kate said with an admirably straight face.

'Alice, give me a hand a minute will you,' her mum said and headed out to the kitchen.

'Which one do you want?' Alice asked when she caught up. She waggled them in front of her.

Her mum pointed to her right hand. 'That one probably, but it's up to you.' She handed Alice a tiny box, the kind in which you'd expect to find a ring. 'You know what it is, don't you?'

'No... unless...' She opened the box. 'Gran's ring! Where did you find it?'

Their grandmother had promised Alice and Kate their choice of her jewellery when they turned twenty-one. Kate was given the locket she'd wanted and always wore it. Gran had died not long before Alice's twenty-first and the ring she'd loved was missing when they went through her things.

'It was in amongst the cards and letters she kept. I didn't look at them until recently; it was too painful.'

Alice hugged her mum.

'I'm all right, love. Anyway, the ring was with all the cards you gave her and your school photos. I'm guessing it was her way of making sure you got it.'

Alice slipped it on. 'Perfect fit! I must have lost weight in my fingers because it only used to go on my thumb.'

'Daft child, we had it resized for you. Don't tell me Kate actually managed to get your ring size without you realising she was up to something?'

'Er, no. Not quite.'

'Well, as you're here, help me carry out the first course, will you?'

The starter was a selection of finger food eaten in the lounge and the party played charades in there between courses to limit the amount of time squashed around the dining table. They were quite squashed in the lounge too, but no one seemed to mind.

The charades teams were the Petes and Peters against the rest of the world.

'If you don't mind, I'll appoint myself an honorary Peter and join your team to even things out,' Petra suggested. She further evened things by being a very good guesser and calling out the answers no matter which team was in play. As Alice's mum was the one keeping score and she spent a lot of the time in the kitchen that didn't matter at all.

Tony was surprisingly good at charades, despite being a little bemused by the complete lack of rules or structure in the version played by the Bakewells. He adapted though, even setting off his musical socks at one point, in an attempt to provide an extra clue.

'I'm impressed those still work,' Kate, who'd given them to him the previous year, said. 'It's almost as though you've not being wearing them on a regular basis, Tony.'

'I've been saving them for best,' he said. Then moving a little closer to her and Alice whispered, 'I think of them as sprout wine.'

The three of them laughed so hard that some kind of explanation seemed in order. They didn't give one. Nor did they explain why they each giggled when one of the others helped themselves to sprouts, or offered the dish to their neighbour. The amusement seemed infectious until every time anyone said, 'Can you pass the sprouts?' a guffaw of laughter resulted. Naturally that meant sprouts were the most popular vegetable and the dish was soon emptied.

'You were right about the sprouts, Janice,' Alice's dad said to her mum. 'I was sure we had plenty. I'll have to grow more next year.'

If he was surprised at his family treating that remark as hilarious he didn't say.

After the meal, Alice's dad and uncle Nigel carried her mum into the lounge. They placed her in a comfy chair and put a glass of wine in her hand, raised her feet onto a stool, forbid her from moving and went to start the clearing up. That, they explained was man's work.

'I'd be happy to help,' Kate's Pete said.

Tony too offered his assistance.

'Thanks,' Alice's dad said. 'We'll add you both to the rota then.'

As plates were washed and the dining room restored to order, gifts were exchanged. This was the traditional routine. As usual most of them were joke gifts, or nice food. Alice's mum always kept a supply of wrapped shortbread and bars of chocolate in case anyone seemed to be receiving fewer gifts than the others. Petra gave everyone a hand embroidered bag type thing. They each thanked her politely and exchanged glances. Alice, along with everyone else she was sure, had no idea what they might be.

'I hope they'll be useful,' Petra said.

Various people said they were sure they would be, then the room fell silent.

'Oh!' Alice heard Tony exclaim. He took his phone from his pocket and dropped it into the decorative bag.

Everyone else quickly followed his example. Petra beamed.

The computer Tony gave Alice was powerful, had extended battery life and came in a really nice carrying case. She had no moment of puzzled surprise wondering what it could be, but neither did she have to fake the certainty that it would be useful.

Tony wasn't in the room when Kate gave her a Hampshire Fire Service calendar.

'Ah so that's where you sneaked off to when I was setting off his siren!' Alice said.

'Yep. Have a look at May.'

Alice flicked through the pages.

There was Hamish, wearing only boots, shorts and helmet. He was holding a kitten it seemed he'd just rescued from a tree.

'Very cute and the cat's nice too.'

She hadn't realised Tony was back in the room or she'd have quickly slipped it into the envelope.

He took it from her, had a quick look and said, 'Hilarious,

Kate, but we're not putting it up. You'd better give it to a charity shop, Alice.' He dropped it onto the pile of other gifts at her feet, then returned to the kitchen.

'Sorry,' Kate said. 'It was just supposed to be fun.'

'I know that and I'm sure Tony sees the funny side really.' She didn't imagine that last bit sounded any more convincing to Kate than it did to herself.

## Chapter 5

Tony didn't mention the calendar again and Alice tried to put the fuss he'd made over it out of her mind. He'd over-reacted, but ever since she'd told him about her slight thing for firemen, he'd been rather sensitive where they were concerned. She didn't want something so trivial to spoil an otherwise lovely day. She was helped with that by Petra suggesting they sing Christmas carols. Alice's dad had a CD of Christmas songs, including a few popular carols which he played as an accompaniment. Alice was amazed that Tony not only joined in, but did so loudly enough to be easily heard despite still being up to his elbows in sudsy water, and well enough that the volume was a good thing. It was almost a shame they didn't stay at the Tatisuz party long enough for him to take part in the karaoke, he'd have been a hit.

It was already Boxing Day by the time she and Tony gathered up their gifts and the box of leftovers her mum had packaged for her. Uncles Pete and Peter dropped them off at Alice's flat, saying they hoped to see Tony again.

'I'm sure you will,' Tony said.

Alice was too tired to do more than blow her uncles a kiss, stagger up to her flat, put the food in the fridge and get into bed. Her head was slightly delicate the next morning. She gulped down a glass of milk. That and a good dose of carbs would soon sort her out. As she activated the microwave she remembered what the uncles had said and realised that if they did meet Tony again it was likely to be the following Christmas. She supposed that if she and Tony were still together then, they would be living together.

Just as she was wondering about her mental 'if', Tony, wearing a dressing gown, came into the kitchen. 'What are you making? Cinnamon porridge?'

'Eurgh, no! Why would I be making that?'

'That's the only breakfast item I could think of which would smell spicy and be cooked in the microwave.'

The oven pinged and she took out the steaming bowl. 'Christmas pudding. Want some?'

'I don't know.' He looked in the bowl. 'It really is Christmas pudding! Why are you heating that up?'

'It's disgusting cold.'

He gave one of his trying to be patient sighs. 'What I meant was, why are you heating it up right now?'

'Because now is when I want to eat it.'

'You cannot eat Christmas pudding for breakfast, Alice.'

'Yes I can, watch me.'

'I will not. Give it here.' He tried to take it from her.

'Step away from the pudding, Tony.'

He let go and stepped back a pace.

'You know where the fridge and cupboards are. Help yourself to breakfast. That's if I've got anything you consider acceptable.'

Just to annoy him she added three large spoonfuls of brandy butter to her dish. It made the whole thing far too sickly. She wasn't going to admit that, so forced it down. Tony sat opposite her, munching on an apple. She'd bought them cheap on the market and although they looked nice she knew they were woolly textured and tasteless. He couldn't possibly be enjoying it. When he'd finished he made them both a coffee. She'd have preferred tea, she usually did in the morning, but she kept quiet and drank the coffee. Her headache improved, but not her mood.

She didn't want a relationship where what to have for breakfast was a source of conflict. She didn't want to live somewhere she couldn't hang her own choice of calendar on the wall and she didn't like the way he'd assumed he knew her answer about moving in with him a week before she was due to give it. Kate was right, seeing less of Tony, not more, might be a good idea.

'I'm going for a shower,' she said. As she allowed the soothing water to flow over her, Alice thought about living with Tony. She'd not really done that. She had of course weighed up the advantages and disadvantages, but she'd not really thought about what it would actually be like to live with him and spend all her free time with him. Or rather all his free time as she'd spend a lot of time on her own waiting for him to finish work. The more she thought about it the more sure she became that she didn't want to do it.

She waited until he'd had his own shower and was dressed before saying, 'Tony, I said I'd give you an answer by New Year, but I've already decided I'm not ready to move in with you.'

'Oh? What do you get up to that you don't want me knowing about?'

'Nothing. It's just that I like a bit of space sometimes.'

'What's that supposed to mean?'

'Just what I said. I want to have mad things for breakfast

without explaining myself, or buy a pretty cushion I like even if it doesn't match the curtains. I don't want to have to tell someone whenever I leave the flat and give an account of where I've been and who I've spoken to when I get back. And I don't want to put up with you getting moody whenever I don't immediately agree to whatever you want.' She knew she'd left it a bit late to say a lot of this, but once she'd started it wasn't as difficult as she'd imagined. 'Oh, that cleaner stuff you use in the kitchen? Absolutely hate the smell of that and it gets in all the food. I never want to smell it again and I don't want to sit around waiting for you to come home from work, either. Here, Kate can pop in on her way home for a chat...'

'I've never said your sister can't visit you. She'd be welcome anytime.'

'No she wouldn't. You'd tolerate her, just as you tolerate me going to the pub with my old school friends.' Alice only met up with Melanie and the others once a month or so and other than work or seeing her family it was the only thing she did without him. Even so, somehow he always managed to want her to go out with him that night, or to otherwise find it inconvenient.

'You sulk from when I arrange it to when I come back, pretty much as you're doing now, pretty much as you do whenever you don't get your own way.'

He didn't deny any of it, didn't even offer to switch to squirting the kitchen with a different brand of disgusting chemicals. Instead he said he was going to go home and catch up on some work, which she felt rather proved at least one of her points.

Tony hardly contacted her for days. Alice wasn't too bothered about that, after what she'd said he'd probably still be sulking and no fun to be around. She was however starting to suffer cabin fever. Obviously she'd expected to spend most of the Christmas break with him, so hadn't made arrangements to meet up with any of her friends. Chances are they'd already made plans and anyway, if Tony did turn up or call her to arrange a date and she was out he'd just sulk all the more.

They'd previously arranged to spend New Year's Eve with his family but he'd not mentioned it since before Christmas, when they'd confirmed the arrangements. Was he assuming she'd still go along with his plans, or decided that either she wouldn't or that he didn't want her to? No doubt the answer was clear to him, or he'd have been in touch. She could just call and ask of course, but she'd be expected to apologise first for telling the truth and why should she do that?

Normally Alice got on quite well with his parents but if she and Tony weren't on the best of terms the evening was bound to be awkward. On the other hand she'd left it a bit late to cancel and they would already have made a little card with her name on it, to show where she was to sit, and have carefully worked out exactly how much food to serve. Although not really sure she wanted to go, it was probably best to go along with what was expected of her – whatever that was.

Knowing it was cowardly she sent Tony a text asking, 'What's happening about tomorrow night?'

After several minutes staring at her phone she rang Kate. 'I need to get out the flat.'

Luckily her sister just assumed Tony was working. 'I've booked an aerobics class. Starts in about an hour. Want to see if I can get you in?'

'Go on then.' She'd not got on the scales for weeks, being sure she wouldn't like what they said. She didn't need them to tell her anyway. Tony, when she saw him next, would no doubt ensure she was fully informed about the tightness of her clothes.

As she walked towards the sports' centre Alice noticed a group of boys joking noisily amongst themselves. When she got nearer she saw the smaller one in the middle wasn't finding it at all funny. He looked as though he might have Down's syndrome, but with the others surrounding him and his eyes scrunched up with tears it was hard to tell.

The insults one of the bigger lads were using suggested her guess was right. Then he started pushing the smaller boy.

'Leave me alone. I done nothing to you,' he said and raised his arms as though to protect himself from expected blows.

'Leave him alone,' Alice yelled.

'What's it to you, fatty?' the ringleader sneered.

'He's smaller than you and it's four on to one. You're nothing but a bunch of cowards.'

'Want to make something of it, do you?'

His friends had already stepped back and now moved further away still.

'It wouldn't be fair, not with my training.' The yob didn't need to know Alice wasn't so much as a fluffy pink belt in feng shui.

Whether he'd fallen for her bluff or just realised he was on his own, she didn't know, but with a rather feeble, 'You're mental you are,' he jogged off after his friends.

'Are you OK?' she asked the boy.

'I didn't do anything wrong. Mum said keep away from them but they wouldn't let me.'

'It's not your fault, it's theirs.'

By then another boy had joined them. 'Hi, Martin. Sorry I'm late.'

'Hello, Rap.'

Leaving Martin with his friend, Alice went in to meet her sister. 'Sorry, am I late?'

'No, you're fine. Is something up?'

Alice told Kate about the incident she'd just witnessed. 'I really hate bullies.'

'Yes, me too. Best thing probably is to just keep out their way. Usually though they're insecure or cowards deep down and pack it in if you challenge them.'

As Martin had just told her, keeping out of the way wasn't always possible. She did her best to avoid trouble though, didn't she?

The workout was exhausting but fun. They box stepped, grape-vined and hamstring curled to a selection of mad Christmas songs and every time a move involved their hands going anywhere near their heads they had to splay their fingers like reindeer antlers. Alice reckoned she burned off an extra mince pie just from laughing.

After her shower Alice couldn't find her phone.

'You definitely brought it, did you?' Kate asked.

'I'm pretty sure.'

'Let's see if anyone handed it in then.'

No one had, but the receptionist took Alice's details and Kate's number in case it turned up later.

When she got in, Alice found it. That was a relief, as was the text from Tony saying he'd assumed she wouldn't be coming to his parents' with him and had told them not to expect her. Alice didn't reply, just rang Kate to say she'd found the phone and asked if she could join her for New Year's Eve.

'Of course you can. Dad said he'd leave us some wine.'

'Us? Oh of course, you'll want to be with Pete. Don't worry it was just a thought.'

'Oh no! You don't get out of it that easily, my girl. You come and drink your share. Besides, you probably won't be playing gooseberry. Mum forgot they were going out and invited Petra, and Pete and Peter are coming in for a drink on their way to something or other involving bells.'

'OK, if you're sure. I'll stay and kip on the sofa.' Alice's old room was now her dad's brewery and although it still contained a bed she didn't want to spend a night listening to bottles bubbling away and wondering if they'd explode.

'OK. Will it just be you?'

'Yes.'

'OK. Want to talk about it?'

'Not right now.'

'Alice, you are OK?'

'Yes. Or at least... yes, actually I am.'

'OK then,' Kate said.

'You know, sometimes I wish our phones would get

hacked. Our riveting conversations deserve a wider audience.'

'Not risking it! I'm hanging up now.' She did, but she left Alice smiling.


When Alice arrived home on New Year's Day, Tony was there along with lots of small bunches of mixed carnations. She guessed they were the only flowers he could get hold of. She guessed too that he'd felt as odd at midnight with no one to kiss as she had.

'Alice, I'm sorry. Forgive me?'

'That depends. What do you want me to forgive you for?'

'For trying to push you into moving in with me when I knew you weren't really ready. You've not long moved out from your parents' home and want to get used to that before you make another change.'

That was sort of right, but only part of the problem. 'Anything else?'

'And for smothering you. I never meant to, but I see now I did and how frustrating it must be.'

Alice wondered who he'd been talking to. Clearly it was someone very sensible.

'I know how keen you are on fire prevention,' he continued. 'Guess I got carried away and did a fire blanket impression.'

That made Alice laugh and the fact he seemed to understand what he'd done to upset her and to be sorry about it gave her hope the problem was solved. In fact things were great for a few days. What he hadn't said and she hadn't realised was that being aware of his desire to control her didn't mean he was capable of stopping that behaviour. His jealousy and possessiveness flared up again when she showed him the dress she'd bought for the school reunion.

'Who are you trying to impress? I thought it would just be your old school friends.'

'It will, but that doesn't mean I don't want to look good. Kate thought it was perfect.'

'Kate would. Don't you think it's a bit short?'

'No shorter than I often wear.'

'Yes, but you're with me then.'

'I don't see what difference that makes. Besides, you could have come if you'd wanted to.'

'You didn't sound as though you wanted me.'

Maybe that's because she hadn't. Alice had hoped to talk to all her old friends, not avoid the male ones in case Tony got jealous. And of course Hamish might be there. If Tony knew she was saying so much as 'rotten weather' to her former crush he'd probably make some kind of scene. If he learned, as he probably would, that Hamish was now a fireman he'd have a fit.

'Come if you want,' she said, making no attempt to disguise the reluctance she felt.

'Oh don't put yourself out! And don't wear that dress.'

She got an apology that night and though he said she'd look fantastic anyway, he booked her in to have her hair done just before the reunion. That really was a positive step; him actually encouraging her to look her best even though men other than himself would see the result.

Alice was wearing the dress and almost ready to leave when Tony phoned. 'I'll be with you in five minutes, Alice.'

'I'm going out, remember?'

'Yes and you asked me to go with you. Sorry it's taken me so long to realise I should. You cancel the taxi and I'll drive you.'

Alice rang the taxi company, then she waited. And waited. Almost an hour after he'd called, she was getting worried. He was rarely late, even when there was a good reason, and then he always called to let her know. If he'd had an accident driving over just to take her somewhere he hadn't even wanted to go, she'd feel awful. When he arrived safe and well without a word of explanation she was furious.

'I'd have been there an hour ago if you'd just left me to it.'

'What difference does it make, unless you'd arranged to meet someone?' he demanded.

She didn't reply. She was wondering if his change of mind over the reunion was because it was he who'd arranged to meet someone. Perhaps he'd organised something with former prefect Rachel so he could spend the whole time discussing business and not waste it having fun. Well he could talk to her if he wanted, Alice wasn't the one with issues.

When Tony stopped the car to reverse into a parking space she got out, slammed the door and went straight to the hall. She saw several people she recognised, including Hamish who was rushing for the exit.

'Alice! I can't stop to talk as I've been called to a big fire.' He pulled a piece of paper from his pocket. 'Call me, you know, if you want.' He was already running towards the car park as he called the last few words.

When Tony caught up with Alice he said, 'Did you see that idiot?'

'Idiot?'

'He's that fool who couldn't find a cash point, isn't he? Nearly knocked me over! Selfish or what?'

'Selfish? You call a fireman going on duty selfish?'

For a moment, Alice felt mean for snapping. How was Tony supposed to guess the man hurrying out of her school reunion was a fireman going on duty?

'A fireman? Oh now I get it, you came here to meet him, didn't you? No wonder you didn't want me here.'

'Don't be ridiculous, Tony.'

'What have you got there?' He grasped her wrist and took the note. '*Dear Alice, give me a call if you're ever free for that drink.* He's written his number as though you don't already know it!'

'Actually I don't, so please give it back.' She tried not to look at the crowd forming around them.

'No girlfriend of mine is going to phone a fireman!' He didn't so much shout as scream.

'No? Your ex is most definitely going to though. Give me the number, Tony.'

'It's either me or this piece of paper, Alice.'

'Give me the number, Tony.'

He screwed it up and dropped it into the mud, reminding her of the way he'd dropped the calendar Kate had given her onto the floor. She did what she should have done then and picked it up.

Tony strode away. If he noticed the cheers and clapping directed at Alice, he didn't react.

Alice turned to her schoolmates. 'Well, I've just split up with my boyfriend. What's new with you guys?'

Alice's old friends took her to get a drink. She was pleased to find Kate near the bar.

'There you are. I was starting to think something had happened to you.'

'Something has.'

There was laughter as those who'd seen the whole thing gave greatly embellished details to those, including Kate, who'd missed the fuss. Alice noticed Rachel on the edge of the group. It didn't matter that she couldn't hear, she was bound to prefer Tony's version.

'Handsome Hamish is a fireman now, did you know?' Melanie asked.

'I did and I have his phone number!' Alice waved her paper trophy.

'Will you be ringing it?' Kate asked.

'I might.'

'That's a yes,' was a sentiment shared by most of those who'd been Alice's friends.

## Chapter 6

Tony sent her a huge bunch of sunflowers the next day. They were gorgeous, but didn't make Alice smile. Neither did the note saying he was sorry and would make it up to her. It felt like she was trapped in a revolving door of arguments and apologies. She wasn't though, she'd stepped out and left the door spinning behind her.

Once, several months ago, Alice had caught Tony with her phone in his hand. He'd claimed he'd seen it on the table and was simply putting it in her bag so she didn't forget to take it with her, but she'd been sure he was checking it to see who she'd called, or had called her. He'd do it again, wouldn't he if he knew she was in possession of a fireman's phone number? He'd never trusted her, despite not once having a reason to doubt her. To think she'd turned down the opportunity to live out her fantasy of being rescued by a fireman just because there was a chance he'd learn of it and be upset. And why would he have been upset? No doubt he'd have a string of plausible sounding reasons all boiling down to two things, he didn't trust her and wanted to control her.

For a week she ignored his calls and texts and refused to let him in when he called. She also refused to accept the next bouquet he sent. That amount of fragrant lilies, long stemmed roses and lush ferns would make it difficult to move round her flat and she didn't want to feel as restricted in there as she had in her relationship with Tony. They were far too lovely to go to waste though, so she took off the card and asked the delivery girl to take them to the flat opposite.

'Her name is Doris. Just say they're from someone who wanted to make her smile.'

Alice smiled herself as she listened to her elderly neighbour first say there must be a mistake and then thank the girl profusely once assured they really were for her. Alice would make a point of visiting Doris and her little dog later on, to give her a chance to show them off. Doris was always thrilled to receive postcards and made Alice read any she got, so it was easy to guess she'd be delighted with the flowers. The card from Tony went in the bin without being read.

Tony's calls became more frequent, both to her phone and at work. There she had no choice about answering but she hung up as soon as she realised it was him. When both Kate and her parents began to get calls she realised ignoring him was just passing the problem onto someone else and she answered the next time he phoned. As soon as he let her speak, she said. 'It's over, Tony.'

'You don't mean that.'

'Yes. I do. I'm going to pack up everything of yours that's here and bring it over. I'd be grateful if you could have my stuff ready to collect.'

'Has Kate put you up to this? You don't have to do everything your big sister tells you, you know.'

She clenched her teeth and breathed deeply. 'When would it be convenient for me to collect my things?'

'For God's sake, Alice!'

'When, Tony?'

'I'll bring them tomorrow evening.' After a pause, he added, 'I really am sorry, Alice.'

'I know.'

She didn't want to be on her own when he came and have to listen to more apologies or pleas for her to change her mind. Having Kate with her would probably turn an awkward situation into a row and she didn't want that either, so she phoned her mum.

'We'll come over, love. Don't worry about it.'

When they arrived Kate was with them, but she'd only come to take Alice out until after Tony had been.

'If you see him it will probably be upsetting for both of you,' her mum said. 'We'll call you when he's been and gone.'

'So how are things with Pete?' Alice asked her sister once they were settled in the pub.

'Fine thanks.'

'Fine? That sounds like something I'd have said about Tony. Is it not going well or are you trying to spare my feelings?'

'You know me, always tactful!'

'Hmmm. So it is OK? Come on, spill.'

'He's lovely.' There was no doubt she meant it.

'You don't talk about him much.'

'No.' She sipped her drink. 'Alice, now might not be the time, actually it's obviously too late, but think about the things you told me about Tony. Who were you trying to convince when you kept saying he wasn't smothering you, or that he had lots of good points or that actually you'd gone off all your favourite clothes and preferred to dress in a burkha?'

'It wasn't as bad as that... but you're right, we weren't right for each other and deep down I've known that for a while.'

'So, Handsome Hamish? You're going to call him, right?'

'Probably.'

'Do it. Nothing mends a broken heart like hot sex with a member of the emergency services, take it from me.'

'I'm not sure my heart is broken.' Admittedly the cure sounded tempting. Maybe it would work as a preventative, but Alice wasn't sure Kate really knew what she was talking about. 'When have you ever had hot sex with an emergency services guy?'

'Don't you remember Malcolm?' Kate asked.

'No... the only Malcolm I remember you seeing was that spotty bloke who worked for the AA.'

'That's the one. Huge spanner and he could jump start anything!'

They had a text, saying Tony had left, before Kate's pep talk could get any more detailed and attract any more of a 'pretending not to listen' audience.

As well as the things she'd left at Tony's flat, he'd brought more flowers.

'You shouldn't have taken them,' Kate said.

'It wasn't my place to refuse and he really is sorry,' her mum said. 'I think he understands now where he went wrong.'

'Wouldn't stop him being just the same within a week though, would it?' Kate asked.

'No, probably not. I didn't mean you should change your mind, Alice, just that I couldn't help feeling a bit sorry for him.'

Alice said, 'You take the flowers, Mum. They'll look lovely in the lounge.'

'OK, love.'

Her dad offered to change her lock, but after checking he'd returned her key, Alice said it wasn't necessary.

When she got home from work the next day and saw Tony waiting outside she began to wonder about that.

'I just came to bring this,' he held out one of her necklaces. 'I missed it when I packed up your other things.'

No he didn't. It would have been with the other two which he'd already returned. Nothing was ever out of place in his tidy flat. He'd kept it deliberately as an excuse to come back. She wasn't going to argue with him though, not any more.

'Thanks,' she took it from him, then climbed the stairs and tapped on Doris's door. She didn't look back to see if he followed, but when she came out half an hour later after making a fuss of Rufus, her neighbour's dog, and drinking a cup of tea, he wasn't to be seen.

Alice didn't hear from Tony again until Valentine's Day when he sent her a pretty posy of scented blooms. The attached card read 'I miss you'. He'd signed it and added a single kiss. It made her cry. She considered sending a message to thank him, but decided it would be better not. His birthday was in April, perhaps she'd send him a card then to show there were no hard feelings.

She waited another two days before calling Hamish.

After a few minutes chat about the reunion and regret he'd had to leave so early, Hamish asked, 'So, no boyfriend now?'

'Hmm.'

'You don't sound sure.'

'I'm sure it's just... how about I tell you when I see you?'

'OK. Tonight at the Sunken Yacht?'

'Works for me.'

'See you about seven then?'

It took Alice a long time to decide what to wear; there was so much to take into account. It was a first date so obviously it was important she looked good. A first date with a fireman she'd once had a crush on, and apparently still did, which took it two stages up from important. Crucial? Vital?

Then there was the weather. It wasn't exactly warm out and she'd be walking to the pub and possibly home again after one drink. Thinking back over the conversation she wondered if all he had in mind was a kind of pre-date chat to see where he stood. She'd get on better if she stopped thinking about what was in his mind and concentrated on what was in her wardrobe.

Her pleated skirt was quite smart and the Sunken Yacht was a fairly smart pub, so she'd wear that. It was on the short side but if she wore thick tights and boots against the cold, that should stop her looking like a complete tart. Well it would if she opted for the sensible boots she could actually walk in. Yes, they'd be perfect – they had furry turnover tops in the same dark grey as her skirt. A white blouse on top? No, too much like school uniform and she didn't want to give the wrong impression. In this case the wrong impression would be of an awestruck fourteen-year-old with mild acne; exactly how she'd been whenever she came in contact with him in fact. Besides, she didn't want him thinking she was so uniform obsessed she wore one herself.

Her black velvet top? No, it'd seem borderline goth with the rest of her outfit. The pale yellow? No, she'd freeze. A cream blouse might be OK, that would go with her woolly tights so she'd be super co-ordinated and classy. And if she put something colourful over it then it wouldn't look like school uniform. Her mad orange jumper with the 3D knitted oranges complete with black stalks and vividly green leaves? It wasn't what anybody would consider appropriate dress for any occasion she could think of, but it was colourful and it was cosy. She pulled it on. If anything it looked even more mad once contrasted with the crisp pleats of her skirt.

This was hopeless. Maybe she should ask Kate's advice after all. She picked up her phone and saw it was a quarter to seven. Yikes! She tugged on her boots and rushed down the stairs and out the flat doing up her coat and stuffing her hands into her gloves as she went. Women weren't objects to be judged solely on appearances anyway, were they?

Hamish already had a drink in front of him when she arrived at the Sunken Yacht. He got up to give her a peck on the cheek and a hint of his citrussy aftershave. Alice resisted looking at her phone to check the time or just apologising for being late in case she was. He'd said about seven and it must be somewhere around that time.

They went through the conventional, 'nice to see you', 'can I get you a drink?' and 'where shall we sit?' in a rather stilted manner. That could be good though, couldn't it? If she was just some girl he was having a drink with because he happened to have gone to the same school as her, he'd be chatting as easily as he had on the previous occasions they'd met, wouldn't he?

Alice removed her coat and hung it on the back of a chair.

She saw Hamish had noticed her jumper. His lips twitched and sea-green eyes sparkled as though he'd thought of a good joke and was trying to resist saying it.

'So, Alice, there's something I'd like to get straight.'

Was he wondering if she were the new man from Del Monte? She'd certainly find it easy to say yes to him.

'The boyfriend situation. You were on your own at the reunion and you phoned me, so I'm hoping he's now an ex?'

'Yes. Definitely.'

'That's OK then. You didn't sound so sure this afternoon.'

Alice explained her break-up with Tony was very recent. 'He was possessive and wanted me to move in and... it was all a bit intense. I guess I'm still adjusting to being able to do what I like without having to get approval first and check in afterwards.'

'So you don't want to get involved with anyone for a while?'

Looking at him she did want that very much, but maybe it wasn't a good idea to jump from the frying pan into the arms of a fireman? 'I don't know.'

'Let's just see how things go. If you want space, just say.'

She nodded. Already she felt more comfortable. 'So when did you decide to become a fireman?'

'When did you develop a thing about them?'

She thought of denying it, but instead said, 'I asked you first.'

He put his hands up in surrender. 'They came into school once, do you remember?'

'Oh, yes. There were three of them, an older guy and two

younger ones who were actually quite...' Too much information, Alice! Hamish probably wasn't interested in their eye colour and inside leg measurements. 'Er, yes. I do vaguely recall that.' She should as she'd been partly responsible.

'All the classes had safety talks I think and got to set off extinguishers,' Hamish said.

'Yes, we did that. There was a big pan of oil that went everywhere. It could have doubled as a healthy eating lesson as none of us wanted to go near a deep fat fryer after that.'

'Sixth formers learned about other types of safety too, on the roads and building sites and things and had a careers talk. Learning about all the different roles, and I admit seeing how the girls reacted to a man in uniform, got me interested.'

'And is it how you imagined?' Alice asked.

'Pretty much. There are boring bits; paperwork, constant checks of the equipment and all kinds of regulations and things we have to learn, but all jobs have their downsides.'

'Mine certainly does.'

'A shout is a real adrenaline rush and I love it. It's draining though, even when it all goes perfectly, but it doesn't always.' He went quiet and Alice squeezed his hand, wanting to offer comfort but not knowing how.

After a moment he looked up and gave her a wicked grin. 'Anyway, you and your firemen fetish?'

'It's not a fetish!' Although she knew he was teasing, she threw a beer mat at him.

'Guess it's because that's what's needed to deal with your

fiery temper?'

'Huh! Actually it's because I thought, wrongly as I'm just learning, that members of the fire service were gentlemen.'

'You've not met Red Watch yet! But if it's a gentleman you want, Hamish Mustarde Esq. at your service.' He stood and gave her a bow.

'Oh go on then,' she said, handing him her glass.

He laughed. 'Suppose I asked for that. Same again?'

'Please, but I'll get it.' She reached for her bag.

'A gentleman would never allow such a thing.'

When he walked to the bar, half the female heads in the pub turned to watch. As he waited to be served he chatted to a redhead who was also buying drinks. She giggled and touched his arm. Seeing that and the way Hamish seemed used to such a reaction, Alice felt a sudden stab of empathy for Tony and his jealous streak.

When Hamish returned with their drinks she told him about the time she'd been walking her dog, off the lead, near a building site.

'Frodo was usually well behaved and a real softy, but he ran after a squirrel or something. I heard him whining and thought he was hurt so ran after him. He was fine when I found him, or would have been if I hadn't jumped up next to him and sent us both crashing into the foundations.'

'I'd forgotten about that. You broke your leg didn't you?'

'I did. The fire brigade rescued me and Frodo. I'd got really cold and lost a fair bit of blood and was convinced we were going to die by then, so you can imagine they made quite an impression.'

'So did you. Devon's still nervous of dark-haired schoolgirls.'

'Devon?'

'The guy who lifted you out.'

She thought back to the strong black man who'd rescued her. 'You know him?'

'My watch manager.' He was trying not to laugh though, so hopefully he was kidding.

They talked for hours about music, food and reached a stalemate on whether snooker was really a sport.

Hamish walked her home, saw her up to her door and kissed her cheek. 'Can we do this again?'

'I'd like that.'

'Lunch on Sunday?'

'I can't, sorry.' Her parents and Kate were coming round and inviting him to meet the family on their second date didn't quite fit in with her request to take things slowly.

'OK.'

'I really do want to see you again though. Whenever you have an evening free.' Hardly playing it cool, but better than him thinking she was fobbing him off.

'Evenings are pretty tied up the next week or so. I'll give you a call, OK?'

He gave her another peck on the cheek and was gone.

Overall she thought it had gone pretty well. He'd been very easy to talk to and he'd said he wanted to see her again. As long as he hadn't gone into a huff about her not being available on Sunday and did actually call, she was optimistic about the future. If he was inclined to sulk over it, well she'd been there, done that, and wasn't going through it again even for an incredibly gorgeous fireman. One who was easily big and strong enough to put her over his shoulder and carry her away and... That rather pleasant thought was interrupted by a call from Kate.

'I guess you're home, or you wouldn't have answered.'

'I am, yes. Hamish walked me back, but didn't stay or anything.'

'I should hope not! A nice girl doesn't get up to any 'or anythings' until the second date at least. Talking of which... there's going to be one?'

'Hmm, he suggested lunch tomorrow.'

'OK, I'll be on best behaviour, but my best isn't good enough to stop Dad bringing wine.'

'That's why I haven't invited him. I'm going to bed now, the details will have to wait.'

Leaving Kate to look forward to hearing more about her first date, Alice got ready for bed imagining what might happen on the second... or maybe third, because she really was a nice girl.


The next call suggesting a date came three days later, while Alice was at work. It was Tony not Hamish calling though.

'Please give me another chance, Alice.'

'No, Tony. I'm seeing someone else now.' She hoped that was true.

'Who?'

'That isn't any of your business,' she snapped before disconnecting.

'Alice,' Miles Molde said, making her jump. 'That's no way to talk to a customer.'

'I wasn't talking to a customer, Miles.'

'Oh? And yet it doesn't seem to be your lunch break.'

Tempted as she was to point out she didn't actually have any work to do and she'd not been using a company phone, Alice kept quiet. Talking back to Miles never did anyone any good.

'Still, maybe I should be grateful you're at your desk.' He gestured to the empty positions. 'Where is everyone?'

'Gone for a smoke.' They'd been gone half an hour, and only one of the three smoked, but Alice didn't say so.

'They didn't pass my office.' He walked over to the fire exit which had been wedged ajar and slammed it loudly.

Soon there was a gentle tap and a hissed request to open up. Miles complied and then gave the alleged smokers a long and loud lecture on the behaviour he expected from his staff. It included the unfairness of expecting others to cover for them and disciplinary warnings, which he promised would be followed up in writing.

'Alice, come with me and I'll dictate them. That's if you're not too busy?'

When she returned from that unpleasant task, Kath, Emma and Lucy immediately stopped talking.

'It's not my fault,' she protested. 'If I'd argued he'd just have got someone else to do it and been even more annoyed.'

'It's not that, we've just been talking about the orders,' Kath said.

'Not much to say, we're not getting any.'

'No, but delivery costs have gone up massively.'

'What does that mean?' Alice asked.

'We don't know, but it's odd and Miles is behind it so it's probably bad.'

## Chapter 7

It was two more days before Hamish called Alice. She didn't just sit around waiting though. She was beginning to see that was a mistake she'd made with Tony and was in danger of repeating, especially now Kate spent so much of her time with Pete. Pretty much all Alice's life her parents, elder sister, friends and boyfriends had made the plans and Alice had gone along with those things she either wanted to do, or was pressurised into accepting. On the evening after her date with Hamish, when she'd kept checking her phone in case he'd called, she'd promised herself to change. She'd made a start. Nothing truly amazing, just arranged to meet those of her school friends who could make it for a pizza one evening and gone to an aqua aerobics class on her own because no one she'd mentioned it to had fancied the idea. Actually she hadn't really enjoyed that, but it felt good to be making a few decisions herself and be free to make her own mistakes.

Hamish's call came just after she'd got in from work. 'Still a fan of the fire service?' he asked.

'Absolutely.'

'And still like Chinese food?'

'I do.'

'Saturday night at Tang's then?'

They arranged to meet outside at seven thirty, which meant she had time to plan what to wear and ask Kate to give her a lift.

When Alice phoned to do so, her sister decided that meant

she also had time to go shopping.

'I've got plenty of clothes and he's not seen most of them,' Alice pointed out.

'True, but he has seen the orange jumper. You need something to wipe that from his mind.'

'You're going to knit me a dress from kitchen cloths?'

'What?'

'Wiping up orange disasters...? No? Well, never mind.'

'So, shopping yes?'

'Yes.' Did she actually want to, or had Kate talked her round? Of course she wanted to go. 'If you drive us to West Quay I'll treat us to one of those honey cakes.'


Alice had a lie-in before the trip. Kate did not and sent a text to say she was on her way. As a result Alice was wearing minimum make-up and her usually sleek hair, whilst still clean and shiny, wasn't entirely under control.

After a breakfast of honey cakes and coffee, Kate persuaded Alice to try on a dress in fire engine red which fitted her in a way that meant she'd not have dared buy it when she was dating Tony. As she studied herself in the mirror and saw her hair even more dishevelled from removing multiple outfits, she thought that for once she was looking at her real self. That was confirmed when she pulled back the curtain to show Kate.

'It's very you,' her sister said. 'And verrrry seeeexy.'

'Too much so?'

'Could anything be too sexy when you're dating a hot fireman? Besides, less is more!' She gave an exaggerated wink.

'Maybe, but I could look too desperate.'

'Well you don't. Excuse me,' Kate said addressing an elderly woman who'd just walked into the changing room. 'Does my sister look like a tart in that dress?'

The lady, dressed in smart beige trousers and sensible beige sweater and carrying more of the same, first looked startled, then looked at Alice.

'No. No I wouldn't say that.' She stepped into a cubicle and hung the items she intended to try, before returning to the sisters. 'I was once your age and had a figure something like yours, but I'd never have worn such a dress. I rather wish I had.'

'They've got jumpers in that colour too,' Kate said, indicating Alice's dress.

The lady nodded and returned to her cubicle.

'How could you ask the poor woman that?' Alice asked as they queued to pay for the red dress. 'If she turns out to be Hamish's gran or something you're in so much trouble.'

'Relax, she likes you already, and look.'

Alice turned to see the woman was no longer carrying anything beige and was instead looking through a rack of brightly coloured sweaters.

'Do you want me to take you back to your place now or are you coming home for a bit?' Kate asked when they'd had enough of looking round the shops.

'I'll come in for a bit.'

'Good.' She sounded relieved.

'Something up?'

'No. It's just that Mum's baking. No, not that at all actually. Thing is... I'm spending a lot of time with Pete. You know, at his place, and I don't want them to think we're abandoning them.'

'Oh! You've not said much about Pete lately. I wondered if things weren't going so well.'

'They are. Really well, but I didn't want to go on about it when you were having all that trouble with Tony.'

'Aaaw, thanks. Soooo, tell me about the Pete situation.'

'I just totally and completely love him and he's the only one for me. That's pretty much it.'

'Wow.'

'I know. It should be scary, but it's not at all.'

Alice compared Kate's comments on her feelings for her boyfriend with the lengthy justifications she used to give for continuing her relationship with Tony. Clearly the two situations were very different.

'I'm glad.' It was all Alice could think of to say, but it seemed to be enough.

The sisters didn't say anything else until they arrived at Alice's childhood home a few minutes later.

'About the baking,' Kate said.

'Oh yes! What you said about Pete made me forget about that.' She eagerly jumped out the car and walked round to where Kate was still sat, wearing her seat belt. 'You know the rules, first one gets the biggest slice.'

'I'm right behind you.'

'Kate? Look I know I didn't like it when you said I shouldn't change to please Tony, but you were right. If you're trying to diet or something for Pete then you have to stop it! We're neither of us designed to be skinny and... It's not that, is it?'

'No. Mum had what at first seemed a brilliant idea.'

'Go on,' Alice urged.

'She realised Dad didn't really like the wine he made any more than the rest of us did and was only making it to use up surplus stuff from the garden.'

'Hmm, yes. That sounds right.' Their dad was an excellent and productive gardener, sometimes too much so, especially as he hated to waste any of his produce. His family were expected to consume it all in one form or another. It was fortunate he'd not developed this particular enthusiasm when Kate and Alice were little or they might have been put off all green and healthy foods for life.

'So she thought she'd find lots of recipes for preserves and things, but I pointed out none of us eat pickles and chutneys.'

'True, but if it was that or the wine I'd eat some.'

'Me too, but not enough. Still, she then found recipes from the war when stuff was rationed and home grown veg had to be used in place of other things and she's decided to adapt them.'

'Genius!'

'No, Alice. We're talking beetroot cake, parsnip biscuits, courgette bread...'

'Oh. But it might not be so bad. Her carrot cake is totally yum.'

'I hope you're right.' Kate got out the car and they went in.

The whole house smelled sweet, rich and warm. The

cakes and biscuits looked as good as they smelled, but then her dad's wine generally looked as though it might be OK.

Her mum made a pot of tea and told Alice she'd been experimenting with new recipes, but didn't elaborate on the special ingredients.

Alice cut herself a sliver of chocolate cake. It looked rich, moist and tempting, but she didn't start eating.

The piece Kate took was no bigger than Alice's. She didn't lift her fork either.

'What's up with you two?' their mum asked.

'Er nothing,' Alice said. She drank some tea.

The sisters glanced at each other, took a bite of cake and exchanged glances again. They ate another mouthful and another until their small slices were just smears on the plate.

'OK, Mum, you got us!' Kate said.

'I don't know what you mean.'

'About the parsnips,' she indicated her empty plate.

'That one was beetroot, these are parsnips.'

Both girls took one of the offered biscuits and bit into the butterscotch flavoured crunchiness.

'These are fab! And what's that one?' Kate indicated the loaf cake.

'Courgette and ginger.'

The cake was as dense and rich as Christmas cake and even moister, but the colour was pale and the flavour tangy with the bite of ginger.

'I can't decide which is my favourite,' Alice said. 'I think it's the chocolate one, but I'd better have a bit more just to make sure.'

'Me too.' Kate helped herself to a big piece. 'So what's the plan, Mum? You make the cakes while Dad's out and bury the veg under the patio or something so he thinks you've used them?'

Their mum fetched a book and placed it on the table, open at a recipe for chocolate and beetroot cake.

'But... these have really got all those veggies in?' Kate asked.

'Told you Mum was a genius,' Alice said.

'I am and while we're sort of on the subject... if your men ever do something you're not keen on, say making wine from surplus runner beans, just say you don't like it. Slightly hurting their feelings then will be better than lying to them and living with the consequences. Likewise, if they should do that to you, try not to be too offended. When your dad and I were first married I was a terrible cook and he told me so, relatively tactfully. It made me determined to improve.'

'Good advice, thanks, Mum,' Alice said.

'Unless they say you shouldn't breathe without their permission, though,' Kate added.

'There is that,' Mum said. 'Listen when they're right, otherwise give them a good ignoring.'


Kate delivered Alice to Tang's restaurant a few minutes early for her date with Hamish. He wasn't in sight, but appeared exactly on time.

'There he is, thanks for the lift.'

'No probs, have fun.'

Alice waved to her sister, then just as she registered Hamish had appeared from inside the restaurant and before she could wonder why, he pulled her into a hug.

'Great to see you,' he said without releasing her.

'And you,' she murmured into his shoulder. Being in his arms felt good.

'Not that I can see you like this.' He stood back and looked her up and down. 'Very nice.'

He said it like he meant it, but she wasn't totally sure if he was referring to the fire engine red colour, or the way it made the most of her curves.

'The guys will love that dress.'

'Guys?'

'Yeah. Come on, I'll introduce you.' He took her hand and strode into Tang's, steering her to a long table where all but two seats were already filled.

'Alice, this terrible lot are Red Watch. Everyone, this is Alice. Be nice.'

'Nice dress, love,' one of them called. 'If you're auditioning to be our new mascot you've got the job!'

'Ignore Jeff,' Hamish advised. 'J.E.F.F. by the way stands for Jeff Easily Frightens Females.'

'Does not!'

Hamish introduced her to everyone on his watch and the partners of several of them. They were a friendly bunch, leaning over to shake her hand or wave depending on where they were seated.

'And of course you remember Devon?'

'Yes, of course.'

There was now some grey in his tight dark curls and his chocolate brown skin was more lined than it had been when he'd pulled her from the tangle of scaffolding in a building site twelve years ago, but she had no trouble recognising him. So relieved had she been to see his face peering down and hear his voice saying she was going to be OK that she wasn't ever likely to forget.

'Nice to see you again under more pleasant circumstances,' she said.

The fact that no one asked about the previous meeting suggested they'd already heard the story. Some of the teasing during the meal confirmed it and that they knew she had a particular interest in firemen. Everyone got teased in turn though, so she'd have felt more awkward if she'd not been included in the banter. She could have done without Jeff's attempts to create innuendo from the way she licked barbecue sauce off her fingers and fact she could use chopsticks. His comments about the splits in the waitresses' dresses were no more tactful, but mostly it was harmless fun.

The crowd around the table meant little room between each person. As a consequence Alice was pressed close against Hamish. She was conscious of the warmth from his thigh all evening. At one point he put his arm across the back of her chair as he leant to speak to William who was sitting next to her. She got another subtle whiff of Hamish's clean smelling aftershave and completely lost track of what the man opposite was saying to her.

'Sandra's morning sickness any better?' Hamish said.

'She's fine, thanks mate.' William leant forward and stage whispered to Alice, 'You've not met my missus yet, but I know she'd want me to pass on my commiserations at getting stuck with Hamish the Horrible.'

'Alice,' Hamish said, 'Would you mind telling my dear friends about my school nickname?'

'Er, some people called him Handsome Hamish,' she said, hoping her face wasn't clashing with her dress.

Alice felt Hamish's arm drop down onto her shoulders.

William laughed. 'Kids are so sarcastic.'

Alice looked at Hamish to see how he'd react.

He bent his head toward her. For a moment she thought he was going to kiss her. Instead he said, 'If you're wondering if we're always like this, then the answer is, I'm afraid so.'

'I think I can handle it. Years doing battle with my evil big sister have seen to that.'

'You mean there's two of you?' Jeff asked.

'No, there's just one of me.'

'Oh, but... but you've got friends, right? Me an' Hamish could go out with you and one of your friends.'

'That's a good idea,' Hamish said. 'I seem to remember we were going to come up with a plot to punish Kate for something. This would be the ideal opportunity.'

'Hey! That's not fair!' Jeff said. 'I've got my good points you know. My mum told me.'

'Next time you see her, ask her what they are,' William said.

'Tell you what, I'll get her to write them down for you. Anyone got a piece of paper?'

Devon produced what looked like a till receipt for a single

item and it was handed down the table to Jeff.

'Thanks.' He tore off a small corner and passed the rest back.

It took them two hours to eat their way through the mountains of food which was brought to their table. Alice did her bit by consuming spare ribs, smoked chicken, crispy seaweed, three duck pancakes and a fair bit of beef chow mein. Her efforts with the wine were also heroic. After that she couldn't manage her fortune cookie, but did snap it open to learn, 'the stars shine brightest on the darkest nights'.

Outside, Devon said, 'I'm giving Hamish a lift back to Marchwood, can I drop you off on the way?'

'Holbury isn't on the way.'

'Everywhere's on the way to somewhere,' Devon said.

Hamish sat in the back of the car with her and when they were near her flat he placed his hand over hers. She turned it over so he could hold it properly. Hamish saw her to her door. He gave her another lovely prolonged hug and kissed her cheek. 'I'll call you,' he said.

With Devon waiting outside there wasn't time for more. She did her best not to be ever so slightly miffed by that. If the man hadn't saved her life she'd never have been kissed at all.

She'd considered saying something about Hamish not telling her beforehand that she wouldn't just be spending the evening with him, but decided against it. She probably had given him a confused impression of the kind of relationship she'd like with him, so she couldn't blame him for keeping things casual. Besides, it was a good thing that he wanted to introduce her to his friends, wasn't it? She didn't want to seem as though she didn't like them or would try to keep him from them. Maybe she could drop a subtle hint that it was easier to talk when it was just the two of them. If she did it right he might pick up that talking wasn't all she had in mind.

She didn't get the chance to raise the subject as Hamish didn't call the next day, even after she sent a text thanking him for dinner. Nor the next. Her phone was definitely working though; she checked it several times and Kate got through OK.

When he did ring he said, 'Hope you've recovered from your Red Watch initiation?'

'It was fun.'

'It wasn't until you arrived I realised I hadn't actually said they'd all be there. It's just the meal was planned and I know you like firemen.'

'Er, yes.' He was making her sound like some kind of obsessed groupie and she really wasn't that bad. Not quite.

'In that case maybe you can be persuaded to have dinner with me tonight?'

'If you ask really nicely.'

'Please, lovely Alice, have dinner with me tonight.'

'I'd love to.'

'Excellent. How about doing something with me this afternoon?'

Alice was tempted, but she'd already persuaded Kate to meet her at the gym. If he'd wanted to see her that afternoon he should have said so earlier. She was no longer the kind of girl who waited for other people to tell her how to fill her day.

'It's something that'd help work up an appetite,' Hamish said.

Surely he didn't mean...? Just because she didn't need anyone to tell her want to do, didn't mean she wasn't open to a good suggestion if one were offered.

## Chapter 8

Alice giggled. 'Dare I ask what you have in mind?'

'Terrible woman!" Hamish said. "All I meant was I'm going birdwatching and wondered if you'd like to join me?'

'Birdwatching? You mean going out in an anorak and binoculars and um...'

'Watching birds? Yes.'

'Oh. Right.' That didn't sound quite as fun, or warm, as her guess about Hamish's planned method of helping her build up an appetite. She had nothing against birds, in fact they were quite nice, and would have been happy enough to go if she hadn't already arranged to meet Kate. Her sister might not appreciate being stood up for a lesser spotted whatever and Alice needed the exercise. She'd shared a gym membership with Tony at a tennis club near his place, but obviously hadn't wanted to go there over the last few weeks.

'Sorry, I can't. Not this time anyway,' she told Hamish. 'Do you do that sort of thing a lot?'

'Mmm hmmm. I volunteer at Beaulieu wildlife sanctuary.'

'Oh, interesting.' Oh great, she'd reacted as though his hobby was a bit weird and it seemed he was really keen. Actually it did seem a bit of a weird thing for him to be doing, but that didn't necessarily make it bad. Making parsnips into biscuits had sounded very wrong until she'd tried them.

'Maybe I could come next time then?' That wasn't too pushy, was it? At any rate it should hide the fact that she'd had no idea there was a wildlife sanctuary in Beaulieu, despite having lived just up the road all her life. She'd visited the New Forest wildlife park a couple of times on school trips. That was probably the same kind of thing but as the only bits, other than the cutest baby owls, which had interested her, were the gift shop and picnic lunch, maybe she should just keep that to herself?

'Absolutely, they're always keen to have some help from anyone who's interested.'

Eeeek, what had she just stitched herself up for? Should she explain she didn't know anything except for what she'd learned from *Springwatch* and David Attenborough? Still how hard could it be to put out some bird food and write down how much the robins weighed? She'd often put seeds on the bird table at her parents' and keeping track of numbers was what she did for a living and something she was good at. She'd be fine as long as there weren't too many creepy crawlies bigger than her head and all the cutest creatures didn't get eaten by a lion. That probably didn't happen too often in Hampshire.

When Alice got back after a zumba class followed by watching a DVD with Kate, she looked through her wardrobe for something which suggested an interest in nature and the outdoors.

It wasn't just the lack of sensible footwear and anything remotely like tweed which stopped her putting together a country girl outfit. She also realised how daft she was being. For one thing Hamish wasn't likely to be fooled; other than school uniform, the mad orange jumper was the most sensible and practical piece of clothing he'd so far seen her in. More important though was that she didn't want to fool him into thinking she was anything other than her true self. She'd made that mistake with Tony and then caused frustration for herself and disappointment for him when she'd failed to live up to the image she'd allowed him to create.

She'd dress warmly, stylishly and as practically as she could for their date in flat boots, skinny jeans and tight pink jumper. Her retro(ish) and totally fake sheepskin coat over the top would complete the look and it was at least showerproof.

Hamish took her to a pub restaurant in Romsey, one which Alice had never been to before. One thing felt familiar though; the way every woman turned to admire Hamish. As they looked around for a table Alice thought she saw Tony, but told herself it wasn't his kind of place and she must be mistaken. Driving past his road had brought him to mind, that was all. A look at the menu which included several of Alice's favourites and nothing unpronounceable served 'drizzled in jus' further convinced her Tony wasn't a likely customer. She hoped he was somewhere completely different with Rachel. She'd often thought the two of them would make a perfect couple.

Alice wasn't surprised when Hamish ignored the 'lite bite' and vegetarian options and went for the largest steak on the menu, a jug of green peppercorn sauce and side order of cheesy garlic bread. He must need plenty of protein and calories to maintain that tall, broad shouldered muscular frame. Her mouth watered, but only because she was trying to decide between spare ribs and Hunter's chicken. Well it was at least partly that. The chicken won out when she remembered how much mess she'd made the last time she'd eaten ribs. She was bound to make even more of a mess with a whole plate of them than with the few short ones she'd enjoyed at Tang's and sticky red goo dripping off her chin, onto her clothes and smeared up her arms wasn't everyone's idea of a seductive look.

After they'd ordered, Alice listened to Hamish's account of his afternoon on the mud flats. He described his sightings of large flocks of feeding redshanks, curlew and turnstones as well as the more secretive bittern with such enthusiasm it seemed she'd been missing out. Even so, she thought she'd been right to stick to her plans and meet Kate. He might as well know from the start that she was close to her sister and intended to stay that way. It was also a good thing she hadn't just gone along with his plans and abandoned her own, even if initially Kate hadn't been as impressed about that as she'd imagined.

'You could have gone with him, I wouldn't have minded.'

'I know, but we already had plans and I've cancelled on you before to please Tony. I'm not going to be such a doormat in future.'

'Good for you! I'll remind you of that when you've jumped to obey every order from Sandra the sadist at zumba and are collapsed in a soggy heap on the floor.'

She had too, but not right away as it had taken Kate quite some time to get her own breath back.

When Hamish asked if she'd had a good afternoon she'd kept the details to herself and just said, 'Yes, thanks.'

The depth of her knowledge on all things ornithological

was something she probably should share with him though.

'I like those snazzy black and white birds with big orange beaks. Are they oyster catchers?' she said after steering the conversation back to his hobby.

'They are. I like them too. Always look a bit as though they're planning something.'

'Yes, but something nice.'

'Like getting hold of an extra bite to eat?' He stabbed his fork into one of her chips, very much like a bird grabbing at a tasty morsel before the rest of the flock could get to it.

'Something nice, I said!'

'Chips are nice.' He stole another.

She rather liked his relaxed attitude with her and the way she obviously didn't need to put on any airs and graces, but he needn't think she was the kind of girl who never ate a proper meal. She nabbed herself one of his onion rings.

'An onion ring is worth at least three chips,' he informed her as he took two more from her plate.

'Is that right? How about a piece of garlic bread?'

'I'll let you have that cheap as it's probably a good idea if I'm not the only one to eat it.'

She didn't think he was concerned about the calorie count, especially as he took another chip. Him being the only one with garlic breath wouldn't have stopped her from wanting to kiss him, but it wouldn't have been an incentive and she appreciated him thinking of it – nearly as much as she appreciated him thinking of the actual kissing part.

As she took a big, buttery bite she thought Hamish's way of solving this minor problem was so much better than

Tony's. He'd have gone without whatever it was he'd been tempted to order and then made her feel guilty about his sacrifice. Aaargh! Why was she thinking about him and not the gorgeous fireman opposite? A gorgeous fireman who had plans to kiss her. Hmmm yes, that was much better image with which to fill her mind.

As she'd had so much 'help' eating her main course, Alice ordered a strawberry cheesecake ice cream sundae and a second cider shandy to follow. The sundae was served in an absolutely enormous stemmed glass dish, which was piled impressively high. Hamish's treacle tart and custard wasn't exactly a stingy portion, but she'd definitely got the better deal.

She placed her left arm on the table to create a protective barrier around the dish and pointed her long-handled spoon at Hamish in a threatening manner.

'That'd be a no to sharing then?' he deduced.

'I suppose you could have a wafer if you really want it?'

'Oh, I want it.' He said that in such a low husky voice and raised his eyebrows so provocatively that she scooped a little of the ice cream onto the heart shaped wafer before handing it over. He offered her a taste of his tart but she declined.

The ice cream in Alice's sundae was as thick and rich as crème brûlée and contained decent sized chunks of cheesecake, white chocolate and fruit. That pleased Alice. It was always disappointing when added ingredients were chopped so finely the whole thing was a bland mush. In this case the biscuit base to the cheesecake still had some crunch and the pieces of fruit gave a real strawberry burst. The sauce was good too, thick and tangy and layered with plenty of whipped cream.

She'd almost finished her dessert and put down her spoon to gather strength for the final assault when Hamish reached across the table and took her hand. 'Alice, I really like you. I know you don't...'

'Well look who it is!' Tony interrupted, loudly. Very loudly, but not particularly clearly. Obviously it really had been him Alice had seen earlier and it appeared he'd had several drinks since she first spotted him.

Hoping if she was polite he would be too, Alice introduced Tony and Hamish. The men briefly shook hands.

'Good luck with keeping hold of her, mate,' Tony said. 'You'll be OK being a fireman though. Got a real thing for firemen Alice has.'

'Lucky for me,' Hamish said.

'Oh yeah?' Tony swayed a little as he processed that. Then he lurched forward and rested his hands on the table. With his face close to hers, he said, 'Why all the pretence, Alice? Why let me think you were going to live with me when all the time you planned to find yourself a fireman?'

'That's not fair and it's not true,' she said, trying to keep her voice low and calm.

'No? Found him already had you?' Tony was shouting and when he pulled himself upright had difficulty staying that way.

'I think maybe you'd better go and cool down,' Hamish said.

Tony looked for a moment as though getting ready to make more of a fuss, but then shrugged and stumbled away.

'Aaargh! It took a while, but I thought he'd got the message. Why can't he just leave me alone?'

'Has he made a habit of this?'

'No, not this, but he kept phoning and coming round the flat. I've thought I've spotted his car a few times too, when I've been on my way to or from work. Oh, sorry, it's not your problem,' Alice said.

'No, it's his.'

She shrugged.

'Look, it's not your fault, Alice. Besides I can understand him not wanting to lose you.'

She couldn't think of anything to say, but just as she was starting to feel a bit awkward he gestured at the remains of strawberry sauce and ice cream in the tall glass she'd pushed away. 'Finished?'

'Yes, thanks.' Tony had never entirely approved of her eating desserts; he'd probably be pleased he'd put her off finishing this one.

Hamish reached for her hand again. 'Want to tell me what went wrong?'

'It was his jealousy really.'

'Was he the guy you were seeing when you turned me down before?'

'Yes.'

'He's crazy. You made it quite clear you weren't available.'

'I'm glad that's how you see it. I might have flirted a little, but I thought we were just messing about.'

'And I was in uniform next to my big shiny engine?'

'Despite what my sister says, I am capable of resisting firemen.'

'Shame.'

'Firemen in general that is. There's one in particular I'll find it hard to say no to.'

'That's more like it. Assuming he's tall, blond and rather too fond of chips?'

'Sounds a lot like him.'

He grinned, 'Come on then.' He took her over to a squashy sofa in front of a dying but still cosy log fire. 'You wait there, I'll ask the barman to say when our friend has gone. It'd be better all round if he's not waiting outside to see us off, don't you think?'

'Definitely.' That thought had been worrying her.

Hamish was soon back and he sat close to Alice and told her about Snowball; an injured carrion crow he'd help nurse the previous winter. 'He got his foot tangled up in fishing line. There was enough of it free that he didn't drown, but he couldn't escape the cold water or feed himself so he was in a really bad way when we managed to free him.'

'Aaaw, poor thing.'

'Yeah. We treated him like he was a chick to start with, dropping tiny pieces of food right in his mouth. He got some strength back quite quickly and would take food from my hand. It was as though he knew I wasn't going to hurt him. By the time his leg was healed he'd put on enough weight to be released.'

'Was it just you who fed him?'

'Mostly. I was on rest days when he needed the most care

so it was easiest for me to do it. You can't blame me for the name though. My far better suggestion was laughed at.'

'What was it?'

'I can't say. You'll laugh and I'll get a complex about it.'

'Oh go on.'

'No.'

'Please. I promise not to laugh,' Alice said.

'Sausage.'

She, of course, did laugh. It would just have been a slight giggle had she not been trying so hard to keep a straight face. The more she tried to contain her amusement and the more he pretended to sulk the harder she laughed.

Eventually she got herself under control. 'What happened to him, do you know?'

'He's still around. I know they all look much alike, but I'm sure it's him. If he sees me about, especially if I've got food he comes right up to me. He's much braver than you'd expect, even for a bird which hangs around a wildlife sanctuary. Then the other day I had a sausage sandwich...'

At the word sausage Alice started laughing again.

'Well, if you don't want to hear it.'

'No, I do.'

'And you'll listen properly?'

'Yes.' She tried to look serious.

'As I was saying, I had a sandwich. A sausage sandwich.'

It was no good, she was off again.

Hamish did a much more thorough job of kissing her

goodnight that evening. Afterwards he pulled her close and held her as though he had no intention of letting her go anytime soon. She could feel his heart beating as hard and fast as her own and that wasn't the only evidence that he wanted her just as much as she wanted him. Even so he refused her invitation to come in for coffee, '…or something.'

'I'm tempted. Very tempted, but I can see you don't want to be rushing into anything after what you went through with Tony, so I'd better not this time.' He stroked her cheek. 'And you have to get up for work, in what...' he glanced at his watch. 'About seven hours, don't you?'

'True.' She hadn't realised it was so late.

Her fondness for Miles and Tony took a further nosedive as she climbed into her cold bed. She banished them both from her mind by thinking about Hamish. Before Tony interrupted him, he'd been saying he really liked her and she was sure he really had been tempted to come in. Tony! She'd forgotten her concerns about him lurking outside the pub or her flat waiting to cause more trouble. Hopefully he'd realise he'd made a fool of himself and leave her alone from now on.

Her phone buzzed indicating a text. She didn't really want to look, but knew she'd just lie awake wondering if it was from Tony of she didn't.

The message was from Hamish and read, 'Goodnight, Sausage x.'

She grinned and texted back 'Goodnight and thanks x,' then snuggled under her quilt to imagine giving and collecting those x's.

Alice awoke to a thudding in her head. She felt exhausted and her eyes didn't want to open. She'd not drunk that much the night before, maybe she was ill. Gradually she realised the banging was outside her flat. A glance at her clock showed it was three in the morning. The thumping was joined by the barking of a dog.

'This is the fire brigade. Sorry, but the building must be evacuated.'

Alice pulled on her dressing gown and peeped out through the small gap allowed by her security chain. The man in the hallway certainly looked like a fireman.

## Chapter 9

'Sorry, but you have to leave right now. Just fetch any medicines or anything else you might need, put on something warm and make your way to the front of the building as quickly as you can, leaving all doors unlocked please.'

That certainly sounded like something a fireman might say. The flashing blue lights shining up through the stairwell were pretty convincing too. Alice looked back at the fireman. He might well be a nice person and she was sure he'd be physically fit and strong enough to do the job, but not even his best friends would have described him as a hunk. She didn't recognise him from her calendar or as one of Hamish's watch, but his unexciting looks and the fact Red Watch weren't on duty meant neither point was surprising. OK, so she was awake and this was real.

'Is it a fire?' she asked. There was no smoke or heat; perhaps it was a gas leak or something.

'We've had a report of one, so we're checking.'

It must be quite small then, that was reassuring. Alice pulled jogging bottoms and her orange jumper over her pyjamas, grabbed her new laptop and stuffed her purse, phone, chocolate and other essentials into the case. She collected her coat, gloves, hat and scarf on her way out. Ahead of her on the stairs was Doris and her dog.

Once outside they joined a group of people assembled on the grassed area opposite the flats. She and Doris were asked for their names and flat numbers and to confirm they hadn't left anyone inside.

'If you've any information about people being away, or can't see any neighbours you'd expect to be at home, please let us know so we can be sure everyone is out,' a fireman said.

Alice looked around at the others. She didn't know everyone in the flats that well, but she'd probably at least spoken to them all either as she put out her rubbish or collected the mail. Just as she realised the young Asian family weren't there she saw them coming out of the building, carrying the children. She couldn't think of anyone else who was missing and was surprised to see more people behind the family. As they drew closer and gave their names she realised she had seen them before. What a terrible witness she'd make and it didn't say a lot for her neighbourliness either, did it? She tried to make up for that by offering round the chocolate she'd stashed in her laptop case.

'Thank you, dear,' Doris said as she took a piece. 'They do say something sweet is good for shock, don't they?' She did look a little shaky.

'You must be cold,' Alice said and wound her long scarf round her neighbour's head and neck.

Doris smiled. 'That's better, thank you. Luckily it's a still night, but it's awfully cold just stood about, isn't it?'

Alice noticed that Rufus the dog was wearing the little rug Doris put on him when it rained or was especially cold. Other than her pet, Doris had brought out one carrier bag. It seemed to contain nothing but a dog bowl and box of dog biscuits.

A fireman asked again if anyone seemed to be missing from those they'd have expected to see in the building.

'Are Mr and Mrs Thomas from 12b here? I can't see them,' someone called.

'They're in the Canaries.'

'Oh, lucky them.'

Once it seemed everybody had been accounted for, they were told that a 999 call had been made reporting a fire. 'Does anyone have any information on that?'

People shook their heads and pointed out there were no obvious signs of a fire.

'OK, well the building is being thoroughly checked now. Make yourselves as comfortable as you can and we'll let you back in as soon as we can.'

'Can we go to our daughter's for the night?' one couple asked.

'Yes. Anyone who wants to is free to leave, but please let us know. And if anyone thinks of anything, or wishes to speak to any of us confidentially, just yell, OK?'

The couple who'd made the request gave their names, as did a few others. Alice thought about phoning her parents, but she didn't want to disturb them and it seemed quite possible that if she did they'd still be fussing over her long after her neighbours had returned to bed.

Those who'd thought to grab blankets and quilts offered them to children, Doris and an elderly gentleman. Rufus was having a great time, running round in excited circles as he decided who should be allowed to fuss over him next. A few people tried to sleep, leaning against each other on benches.

Most just stood and watched, though there wasn't really much to see.

The firemen used heat detecting cameras and other equipment, conducted a search and questioned the residents. It wasn't exciting. Reality was definitely not living up to her fantasy. Probably just as well as, instead of a silky nightie, she was wearing baggy pyjamas and tatty slippers which had once looked like pink mice. The slippers were a mistake; she could feel them soaking up the damp and cold. They'd be going in the bin tomorrow, assuming she was allowed back in by then. The orange jumper wouldn't be joining them. Without that she'd be unbearably cold.

She sat on a low wall, it wasn't comfortable or warm, but allowed her to keep her feet off the wet grass. After that she must have drifted off to sleep as she imagined explaining to Kate that she wanted to buy a big orange onesie and instead of laughing at such a horrible idea, Kate offered to knit it for her.

'OK, you can go back in,' they were eventually told. 'Seems it was a false alarm or a hoax.'

'People who do that should be prosecuted,' Doris said.

'Sometimes they are.' The fireman who'd given the all clear walked with them. 'Telephone numbers are automatically sent through to control, and addresses for landlines or co-ordination points for mobiles, so tracing them isn't usually too difficult. Calls are recorded and used as evidence, if need be.'

When she reached her landing, one of Alice's neighbours offered hot chocolate to anyone who wanted it. 'Don't know about you, but I don't think I could go back to sleep just yet.'

'Thanks, but I'm already asleep,' Alice said.

She heard Doris say she'd like some, if she could bring Rufus.

'Oh please do. He's such a dear little thing.'

Alice thought it a good thing the fire alarms were above paw height; that dog was having so much fun he'd probably set them off every night if he could.


At work the next day Alice tried to look alert so as not to give Miles a reason to moan. Her friend Kath noticed her baggy eyes and asked if she was OK.

'Just tired.'

'That fireman of yours been keeping you awake?'

'Actually it wasn't all his fault, most of Green Watch were responsible.' Or maybe it had been White or Yellow Watch?

'Details. Now!' Kath demanded, scooting her chair over to Alice's desk.

All three women crowded around as she told them about the night's adventure.

They didn't notice Miles approach until he said, 'Something more exciting than processing orders is clearly going on here, ladies.'

Emma and Lucy slid back to their stations.

'Alice is lucky to be here!' Kath said. 'Her flats could have been burned down.'

'Is that right?' Miles asked.

'Not exactly,' Alice admitted. 'It was a false alarm and the fire brigade came out for nothing. We had to evacuate though and I didn't get much sleep.'

'You do look tired,' he said. 'Maybe you should go home.'

'I'm fine.' She wasn't about to give him a reason to accuse her of being inefficient. He'd sacked several warehouse staff for that already. It wasn't exactly fair; business was so slow that making themselves look busy was everyone's main challenge.

'I don't think you are, Alice. You need to sleep or you'll make yourself ill.'

He was probably concerned she'd have an accident and sue. The stairs from the storerooms to the offices were in bad shape. Anyone not paying attention as they negotiated them was likely to fall.

'I could take a day's leave. It's not your fault this happened.' It wasn't her fault either and she'd already worked two hours, but was too tired to worry about such details.

'Let's call it half a day and I'll take you home.'

'Oh. Thank you.' Maybe she'd already gone back to sleep. Miles never offered so much as a lift to the bus stop when it was raining, even though they usually left at the same time and he drove right by.

As they left the car park he said, 'Is there someone who can collect your car, or will you need a lift in tomorrow?'

'I get the bus to work, Miles.'

'Having trouble with the Audi?'

'Audi? Oh that was my ex-boyfriend's car.' Tony lent it to her for a couple of weeks when he'd been suffering from vertigo and couldn't drive. Miles had taken an interest because he'd been thinking of getting one himself. She didn't know what Tony's had cost but from the fuss he made if anyone parked close enough for a carelessly opened door to make contact with his paintwork, she guessed it was a lot. If Miles had thought it was hers no wonder he didn't think she needed a pay rise or lift to the bus stop. Perhaps they'd misjudged each other.

'Having to evacuate your home must have been alarming,' he said.

'Not really. Just a waste of time.'

'Don't suppose the fire brigade were happy.'

'Probably not.' She told him as much as she could remember of what the fireman had said about tracing hoax calls.

After a few hours' sleep and some time thinking about what she could do to make one particular fireman happy, Alice rang Hamish and explained about her unpleasant night and how, as a result, she had the afternoon off.

'That can't have been any fun. Hope it hasn't put you off firemen?'

'No, of course not.'

'So we're still on for tomorrow?'

'Absolutely.' How could he doubt it? She'd been hoping he'd come round to cheer her up, not trying to delay seeing him again. 'I can't wait.'

He didn't take the hint.

Kate was, she knew, going out with Pete that evening. When Alice had told her about the fire hoax she'd offered to cancel and spend time with Alice, but she'd refused. She wasn't upset or scared or anything, she just didn't fancy sitting in the flat on her own watching TV. Doing that, plus eating home-made cake at her parents' would be a bit better and they'd be pleased to see her. At least she assumed so, they always acted that way and she was most certainly not going to ask her parents if they had a romantic night in planned.

Before visiting her parents, Alice made sure the whole flat was clean and tidy. Hamish hadn't mentioned any particular plans for the following evening, so might be open to suggestion. She already had a couple of films Kath had leant her and nipped down the shop for crisps, dips, beer and popcorn. Then she bullied herself down the sports' centre. If she arrived at her parents' earlier than she would have on a work day, they were likely to ask why and then worry.

Alice gave a rather pathetic performance in the aerobics class but it was probably better than not bothering at all. She still felt sluggish afterwards and thought her eyes looked puffy so had a short nap. Well, what was intended to be a short nap. She actually slept for three hours. Good thing she hadn't told her parents when she was coming. She called them to say she was on her way over, 'If that's OK?'

'Of course it is, love,' her dad said. 'Your mum's watching some dancing thing, but I'll come and get you.'

'I can get the bus.'

'No, it's dark out. I'll come and get you, love.'

It was dark when she walked down the lane from work and got the bus home in winter but she didn't point that out; maybe this was more a case of avoiding an overdose of sequins than an urge to over protect his little girl.

Alice managed to tell her parents about being woken in

the night by the fire brigade without alarming them. Actually they seemed a lot more concerned about butternut squash. Alice's mum had bought one to make soup and used what she didn't need in the very delicious Dundee cake Alice was helping to dispose of. Her dad had been horrified at the price.

'Two quid for a glorified courgette when I grow hundreds of them?'

'They're quite different, Peter. Besides, there aren't any courgettes left.'

'They don't keep through the winter.'

Apparently the squashes would, but took up so much garden space Alice's dad would have to drastically cut back on everything else he grew to accommodate them. Which Alice realised, as she finally caught on to the importance of the issue, meant there would never again be a big enough surplus for wine production.

'You'll just have to buy them then, Mum, as this cake is really scrummy. What was the soup like?'

'I rather liked it. Did you, Peter?'

'Well, yes but then I like anything with that much butter and cream... actually I was surprised at you making it for me.'

So was Alice; his blood pressure was on the high side and her mum was trying to get him to lose weight.

'No butter, no cream, no fat at all,' her mum said just a bit smugly.

'Really? Can I have the recipe?' Alice asked.

'You don't want to go losing weight, love,' her dad told

her.

Alice wasn't so sure. Without Tony nagging her about the tightness of her clothes and keeping them to a strict exercise regime she'd put on a few pounds. She wasn't overly worried about what the scales said, but she'd rather not have to buy new clothes in a bigger size.

'I wonder if you can eat the seeds,' her mum said interrupting her thoughts.

'Had seeds in it, did it?' Alice's dad asked.

She fetched them to show him.

'These might grow you know. Wouldn't hurt to try some I suppose.' He took them from her.

Alice was very impressed. It wasn't just low fat soup making she hoped to learn from her mother. A few lessons on handling men wouldn't go amiss.

That night Alice tried to send herself to sleep by imagining getting Hamish to do exactly as she wanted. It wasn't successful; she kept jerking awake thinking she could hear sirens, or people knocking on her neighbours' doors.

Even more frustrating, when Hamish arrived the following evening he gave her a quick kiss and, before she could suggest they'd be more comfortable if they went inside, said, 'How do you fancy going bowling?'

'Bowling?'

'You know, bowling.' He mimed bowling the heavy ball down a lane as though trying to knock down pins at the end of the landing.

'Sure, if you like.' She had nothing against the game, it just seemed an odd choice for a fourth date. More the sort of thing you might do for the first one or if going out with a bunch of mates. Was this a clue that he didn't want the same kind of relationship as she did?

When she got into his car and saw Jeff and William from his watch in the back, she couldn't decide if that was good or bad. They were on the same wavelength about bowling being something to do with a group, but why did he want them to go out with his friends when he could have stayed in with her? Maybe it was a warning that if she wanted one member of Red Watch she'd have to accept them all.

The bowling was fun but, as she'd imagined, more like an evening with friends than a real date. Hamish picking her up and swinging her round after she scored a strike was as intimate as it got.

Alice wasn't excluded from conversations, in fact Jeff paid her far more compliments than she was entirely comfortable with, but naturally work topics crept into their chatter and there were a few in jokes which meant nothing to her, even after William did his best to explain.

'Getting down and dirty with your birds again tomorrow?' Jeff asked Hamish at one point.

At least she understood that; he was referring to the wildlife place Hamish helped out at.

'Absolutely,' Hamish said. He turned to Alice, 'Maybe I'll see Sausage.'

Once she'd stopped giggling she said, 'I think you'll find his name is Snowball, which as anyone can tell you is a much more sensible name for a crow.'

'I thought crows were black?' Jeff said.

That made both Alice and Hamish grin. It felt good they

already had an in joke of their own.

'I'd like to see Snowball-Sausage.'

'I'm sure he'd like to see you too. Presumably you're working tomorrow?'

'Yep. Monday to Friday, nine to five.'

Hamish explained the fire service's watch system; two twelve hour days, two twelve hour nights and then four days off. 'I've committed two of those four day periods a month at the sanctuary.'

That explained why, although she knew he wasn't working over the weekend, he hadn't arranged to see her between then and Sunday evening.

Alice got a proper kiss goodnight, but just one. His friends, who lived close to him, were waiting in the car.

Her earlier nap, combined with some disappointment over how the evening went, meant she slept badly for a third night in a row.

By Friday Miles was back to his irritating best, having them create profit projections and sales forecasts based on what, going by the recent slump, were wildly optimistic order estimates. He was furious when told the information couldn't be printed out because the only computers which connected to the printer network were no longer operational.

'Why wasn't I told?'

Kath jumped up, sending her chair crashing into her desk, strode into his office and returned with a handful of paper which she thrust under his nose. 'You were! We've all explained and had to fill in your stupid forms saying we're using our own machines.'

For a moment it looked as though he'd explode, but he suddenly calmed down.

'Sorry. I've had a lot on my mind. Ring and get the IT company to come and sort it out, will you?'

'We don't have a maintenance contract any more.'

'Then they'll have to invoice us, won't they?' He returned to his office leaving Kath the difficult task of persuading the IT people, who'd had their contract terminated without warning, to come out at short notice and then bill Tatisuz, a company who were rapidly gaining a name for being bad payers.

Alice wanted cheering up, but sensibly decided to wait until her lunch break to phone Kate. Her sister let her moan about work for a while then asked how things were going with Hamish.

'I'm not sure,' Alice said.

'I was worried this might happen.'

'What would?'

'That once the excitement of dating a fireman had worn off you'd be bored with the man himself.'

'It's not that at all. He's lovely, what I know of him, but I don't seem to be able to get beyond the fireman. He talks a lot about work and socialises with his colleagues and...'

'He isn't putting out your fire?'

'No. Kate, do you think he's got the same idea as you? That I'm only interested in him because he's a fireman?'

'Possibly. Or maybe he's just taking things steady?'

'I may have said something about Tony being too intense.'

As Alice munched her way through a cheese sandwich,

the answer came to her. It was Hamish the bird watcher, not Hamish the fireman she should concentrate on getting to know. She rang his number.

A woman answered. 'He's busy just at the moment.'

'Could you tell him Alice called?'

'Hi, Anna. I didn't recognise your voice.'

'Not Anna, Alice.'

'Oh, a new one. OK I'll tell him.'

Alice didn't believe for a moment that the woman had mistaken Alice for Anna, but she couldn't tell if she was warning her off or just being bitchy.

## Chapter 10

Alice had finished her second sandwich, an apple and a KitKat by the time Hamish called back from the wildlife sanctuary. Resisting the urge to ask who the woman who'd answered his phone was, she said, 'I'm eating my lunch watching starlings eat theirs and wondered what birds you could see.'

'Mostly gulls.'

'No sign of Sausage?'

'No, but he only approaches when I'm at ground level. We're repairing nest boxes and you can guess who they send up the ladder.'

'I can see you'd be handy for that. What else do you do there?'

Hamish told her a little about conservation work, recording information when birds were ringed and building hides.

'It sounds really interesting.'

'Want to join me tomorrow? There's always plenty to do.'

Result! 'Yes, I'd like that.'

'If you're sure? We'll be working all day, not just having a nice day out.'

'That's fine, really. I'd like to do something useful.' She could do with the exercise too. Other than a couple of aerobics classes with Kate and walking up the stairs to her flat and down the lane between the bus stop and work she'd done nothing for ages. She couldn't keep that up without putting serious strain on the seams of all her favourite clothes.

'Great. Is eight too early to pick you up?'

'No, that's fine.' She wasn't usually up that time of a Saturday morning, but then she didn't usually have much reason to be.

'You'll need to wear something warm which you don't mind getting muddy.'

'No problem.' Well it might be, but not one she couldn't solve by eight the following morning.

That afternoon a man from the IT company came out. He confirmed what Miles had already been told by his staff; the only computers compatible with the printer were no longer working.

'We can supply and install a domestic type printer today which will do the job for now, but I recommend updating your entire system.'

'Supply at a mark-up and charge for installing no doubt? Just tell me what I need and I'll sort it out myself.'

'Suit yourself, but we're charging to be here anyway and I have a suitable machine in the van. You might as well have me do something.'

Miles hesitated, but when it was pointed out the printer would cost less than £100, so any mark-up was likely to be less than the cost of driving to somewhere he could buy one, he grudgingly agreed.

'I'll just nip out to the van and fetch it,' the technician said.

'Would you like a tea or coffee?' Lucy asked. It was coming up for three and her turn to make the drinks.

'Grand. Either's fine. Milk and two sugars please.'

After he'd left, Miles said, 'Might I remind you that the tea and coffee are for staff only?'

Alice took the kettle from Lucy and filled it to the top. They all paid in for the drinks, which didn't stop Miles expecting someone to make them for him and any visitors he had. She'd make one for the computer man and if Miles saw and complained she'd remind him of that. Kath would back her up she knew.

The tea was drunk, mug washed and printer installed before Miles returned to the main office to see if progress had been made. The technician proved it was working by having Kath print out an invoice for the job, which he'd just asked to be emailed through.

'If you'd like to give me a cheque now it'll save you posting it,' he told Miles.

'We have a procedure for paying bills,' Miles said.

They did. Just lately that was to ignore them until legal action was threatened.

An hour later a siren was heard. A fire engine, blue lights flashing, pulled up in front of the Tatisuz building. It seemed they'd been alerted by the automatic alarm system. For the second time that week Alice was evacuated into the cold, whilst a fire crew checked for a non-existent fire. Miles was furious, saying he expected the IT company to give him a reduction to compensate for all the time his staff couldn't work.

'Come off it, Miles. We're hardly rushed off our feet and it's been less than an hour,' Kath pointed out.

'It's nearly five now, so I don't suppose anyone will bother going back to work.'

'Thanks, boss. Decent of you,' one of the forklift truck drivers said. He and his mates headed for their cars, seemingly unable to hear Miles saying that wasn't what he'd meant.

'Oh go home the lot of you!' Miles snapped.

No one needed telling twice and everyone got away a good half an hour earlier than usual. Alice walked slowly up the service road towards the bus stop, texting Kate on the way to ask if she could borrow her wellies.

'Sure. They're still at M&D's' she texted back. Kate wasn't officially living with Pete yet, but she spent more nights at his place than she did with their parents and had transferred over quite a lot of her things.

'Thanks. Will call round for them now'.

As she sent the message, Miles pulled up beside her. 'I can drop you off on Long Lane if that's any use?'

'Oh, yes please.' She quickly climbed in. 'I'm going to my parents in Fawley, so the nearest you go to there would be great.'

'Which road?'

'Coleville Avenue.'

'Ah. OK.' Then after a pause, 'What did you think of that computer chap? Bit cheeky eh?'

'Hmm.' She didn't want to argue with someone who'd let her leave work early and was giving her a lift.

'Some people think just because I'm running a business it's OK to rip me off. They don't seem to realise that if I can't keep costs down it's my staff who'll suffer. I really don't want to have to lay anyone else off.'

'No, it must be difficult.'

Kath had said he'd already got rid of everyone he could without having to make redundancy payments, but even if true that didn't prove he'd actually wanted to do it. Alice could see that being responsible for everyone's livelihoods must be a strain. He hadn't been quite so awful before the company ran into financial trouble.

Miles turned into Coleville Avenue. 'Whereabouts?'

'Just by the blue van. Thanks very much.' Alice got out. Just before shutting the door she bent down and said, 'Have a nice weekend.'

'Yes, you too, Alice.'

Alice hesitated on the doorstep. Now she wasn't living with her parents she wasn't quite sure that she should just walk in when they weren't expecting her. Especially as Kate was rarely there and they might reasonably expect some privacy. Knocking and waiting for them to stop whatever they were doing and come to the door didn't seem right either. She let herself in, calling a greeting as she did.

'Is it that time already?' her mum asked.

'We finished work early because of a fire alarm problem and the boss gave me a lift home.'

'Fire alarm? The same as at your flats?'

'No. Well, we got out for nothing, but nobody called the fire brigade. We had some work done on the computers and that did something to the smoke detectors or something like that.' She could only hope all the technical jargon wasn't too complicated for them.

'You've been stood outside in this weather? I'll put the kettle on.'

'Thanks, Mum.' A cup of tea and piece of cake were her mum's cure for just about anything. Quite often it worked.

By the time her mum had brought through mugs of tea and a plate of flapjack, Alice was helping her dad with his garden plan. He rotated his crops so the same type of plant wasn't grown in the same place more than one year in three, which he said kept the plants healthy. Usually it was just a case of shifting things round on his scale drawings, but the planned addition of butternut squash meant major changes.

'I don't know whether to cut down the numbers of everything, or have the same quantities of less sorts.'

Alice knew the answer to that one. Lower quantities of any one thing meant insufficient amounts left over for wine making. 'A bit of everything I'd think, Dad. Like you say, you never know what's going to do best from one year to the next.'

'That's true.'

'Don't go digging up the rhubarb plant though, Peter,' Alice's mum said.

'Don't worry, I won't. That always does well and if we can't eat it all I could always turn it into a drop of rosé.'

'Talking of eating it, try the flapjack.'

Alice and her dad both helped themselves to a piece. Each chunky section had a pale pink layer through the centre. The flapjack itself was crumbly, rich and buttery, the perfect contrast to the tangy rhubarb filling.

'Oh fab, Mum.'

'I wondered if the rhubarb would make it go like porridge, but it seems OK.'

'A lot better than OK.'

'I do like it,' Alice's dad said.

'You like it, but...?' Her mum winked at Alice.

'I still prefer a pie, with custard.'

'Pick me some more and I'll bake you one.'

'It'll be a few days before any's ready and if we keep taking it from the forcer there won't be much later on in the year.'

'No, but we'll have gooseberries then, and blackcurrants. They both make good pies.'

'That's true, Janice. They're good for wine too, but better in pies. Quite a lot of things are better in pies.'

'You're right there, Dad. Especially one of Mum's pies.'

'Flatterer! I suppose you'll be staying to supper then?'

'Well, if there's enough?' Alice tried to look like the kind of innocent daughter who wouldn't have dreamed of angling for an invitation.

'It's sausage and mash so it's easy to do a bit more. Peter, fetch a few more spuds will you?'

'I'll get them,' Alice said. 'I need to go in the garage anyway. Kate said I can borrow her wellies. Where are they?'

'You'll see 'em.'

Her dad was right. Alice had forgotten how bright they were. A hideous shade of yellow decorated with red and blue cupcakes. They were also a bit too big. Three pairs of socks would solve one of those problems, hopefully the promised mud would soon deal with the other. When she explained why she wanted them, her dad leant her a thick coat too. It was a spare gardening one, so getting it dirty wasn't a worry.


Alice was just about ready when Hamish arrived. She saw him give her appearance a hasty inspection.

'Sorry about the boots. I hope they won't scare the wildlife.'

'No they're fine. Actually I'm impressed; I was worried you wouldn't have anything suitable for working in.'

'I don't really, I borrowed the boots and coat. I am willing to work though, just not used to it.'

'I do like a willing girl.' He pulled her as close as her many layers would allow and gave her an unhurried kiss.

She hoped that was just a taste of the reward she was going to get for whatever tasks he had planned for her. And as it was the weekend, she'd be negotiating for double pay.

'I suppose we'd better get going,' Hamish said. There was a pleasing note of regret in his voice.

During the drive to Beaulieu, Alice asked what they'd be doing.

'One plan is to make some new nest boxes. How are you with a hammer and nails?'

'I'm better with an emery board to be honest, but I don't mind fetching and carrying or whatever is useful.'

'There's always plenty to be done, especially if you're prepared for the mud.'

'The more mud these boots get on them the better.'

'You want to be careful making rash statements like that, you could come to regret it.'

Alice walked with Hamish across the car park and into a wooden building with a 'staff only' notice on the door.

'Hello,' he called as he went in.

Someone greeted him and offered coffee. Alice recognised the voice as the one which had answered his phone the previous day.

'Make that two please, Louise,' Hamish said.

As she followed him in, Alice saw the small building was stuffed full of mismatched chairs, a sofa and wooden benches. There were two doors at the far end. One had a sign indicating it was a unisex toilet, the other was open to reveal a tiny kitchen area and a tall, thin woman of about thirty. She didn't look happy.

He introduced the two women.

'Well this is a surprise!' Louise said. 'First time Hamish has brought one of his girlfriends here. You'll know how a kettle works I imagine.' Louise pushed past them and slammed the door behind her.

'I don't know what that was about, she's usually lovely.'

'I think she likes you, Hamish.'

'Of course she does. We've been friends for years.'

Oh great, another Rachel type situation. Except Rachel had been icily polite rather than openly hostile. It was hard to say which was worse.

Hamish made their coffee and then three more mugs when Louise returned with a middle-aged couple. Soon others joined them until every seat was occupied. Hamish introduced her to everyone in turn and she was warmly welcomed, especially when he explained she was there to work and looking forward to getting muddy. They began discussing who would do what.

'Perhaps you'd like to help Louise clearing the mudflats, Alice?' asked a man she thought was called Nadeep and who seemed to be in charge of organising everyone.

Oh help, now what should she say? The woman was Hamish's friend, all these people were, so she didn't want to cause trouble.

'If that's what would be most useful,' she said.

Louise grimaced.

'Are you OK, Louise?' Nadeep asked.

'Fine, I've just got a bit of a headache.'

Alice had some painkillers in her bag, but rather suspected the only way they'd make Louise feel better was if one of them, preferably Alice, were to swallow about three packetfuls.

As the others dispersed, Louise said, 'Well come on, if you're coming.' She went out.

Pulling on her woolly gloves, Alice followed.

Louise sighed, then went back inside the building, returning with a large pair of bright red rubbery gloves. 'Way too big, but waterproof.' She thrust them at Alice.

'Oh, thanks very much. I... I've got some painkillers if it'd help?'

'What? Oh no, I'll be OK when I get some fresh air.' After a moment she added, 'Thanks though.'

Outside the building, Louise opened a plastic tub which was in the corner of a small fenced off area of concrete. She extracted a piece of shiny black plastic.

'So what exactly is it we're going to do with the mud?' Alice asked.

'I'm going to hold you face down in it. You don't have to do anything, but I expect you'll struggle for a bit before you drown.' She didn't say it like it was a joke.

Louise strode away leaving Alice to wonder if following was really such a good idea. The wooden shed was dry, had a heater and kettle and if she died there someone would find her body.

## Chapter 11

'Won't there be witnesses and too many people who know I was with you?' Alice spoke as calmly and reasonably as she could. Probably Louise was just grouchy and not a homicidal maniac, but there was no absolute guarantee of that.

'Good point.' She gave what might have been a quickly suppressed grin. 'OK, I'll just have to kill you with hard work.'

'That'd be easier to explain away.'

'You'd better not be some kind of fitness freak who actually survives this.' She really did smile that time.

With all the layers she was wearing and the way she had to half trot to keep up with Louise's long stride Alice knew she didn't give the impression of being super fit.

'I've been to a gym!' she told Louise.

'Me too. It was bloody awful.'

Louise gave the piece of black plastic she'd collected earlier a shake, revealing that it was two heavy duty rubbish sacks. She handed one to Alice.

'Basically anything manmade goes in there. Bits of wood, even sawn planks or whatever can stay as long as they don't have metalwork or plastic coatings or anything. When it's full leave it outside the staffroom and collect another. Rinse and repeat.'

Although it was tricky keeping them on, Alice was grateful for the gloves even before she put her hands into the mud for the first time. Interesting was the word Alice had used to describe conservation work when talking to Hamish the previous day. It wasn't the one she had in mind after hours spent pulling shopping bags, bottles and fishing line out of foul smelling mud with Louise. Mostly it was just ordinary rubbish, but the thick, smelly gunge clinging to it made everything far heavier. Anything a bit bigger was hard to pull out and when it eventually came free, Alice was sent staggering backwards. Some things were too difficult for one person to shift; Louise and Alice dragged what had probably once been a child's mattress out of the mud and back to the wooden building. Later they did the same thing with a big piece of plastic sheeting.

The other woman wasn't exactly chatty, but she did assure Alice the work they were doing would be very beneficial to the birds and other wildlife who fed on the shoreline and river banks. It was keeping Alice warm too and had to be burning calories.

Whenever Alice stood and stretched to ease her aching back she saw Louise haul out a large piece of debris or throw the full bag over her shoulder and march off towards dry land with it. Alice was reminded of the first time she'd gone with Tony to his gym. A woman wearing pristine trainers, obviously new and expensive workout clothes, and a full face of make-up had taken the rower right beside the one Alice was trying to figure out how to use.

'You'll want to turn the resistance level down I should think,' she'd drawled, then put hers up to ten.

Alice had done the same, then matched the woman stroke for stroke. She was hot enough to believe in spontaneous human combustion by the time the other woman stopped, but somehow found the strength to stand up and make it to the water fountain. Leaning on it for support she'd gulped down a few mouthfuls. The other woman hadn't passed her, maybe Alice would have the satisfaction of seeing her slumped in an exhausted heap? She'd looked round to see the woman pounding away on a treadmill set at a ridiculously steep angle. Alice hadn't been able to lift anything heavier than a coffee cup for days and had learned her lesson. Well sort of. She kept going, but didn't try to compete with Louise's work rate.

Alice knew she'd have stiff muscles the next day, but the exercise would do her good. Treadmills, steppers and rowing machines were nothing compared with the workout she was getting amongst the reeds and willow roots and it went on for hours and hours. At least it felt like it when they stopped for a break and returned to the staff room.

Although desperate for the loo, Alice hadn't liked to say in case Louise thought she was just making an excuse to stop working. Now they had stopped, Alice headed straight into the toilet. Wrestling her way out of enough clothes to make use of it took some time and Louise had a coffee ready for her when she came out.

It was only just gone half past ten! Would she be expected to keep this up until dark? And even more importantly, would there be food? It hadn't occurred to Alice to bring anything with her other than the sausage she'd cooked for Hamish's crow and the emergency chocolate she kept in her bag. If this wasn't an emergency she didn't know what was. She fetched the bar, snapped it in half and offered one part to Louise.

After a moment's hesitation, Louise reached forward and

took it. 'Thanks,' then as Alice turned towards the sofa intending to slump into it, 'Don't sit there, the springs are gone. The big blue armchairs are probably the least uncomfortable.'

Alice crashed into the twin of the one Louise occupied. Not for long though. Louise had finished her drink, used the toilet and was putting on her coat before Alice had finished her chocolate. She gulped down the last of her drink and began covering herself up again. It didn't take too long as she abandoned several layers, confident the work would ensure she didn't get cold. She was right.

Even though fewer layers made it a little easier to move, Alice stumbled several times taking yet another full rubbish sack back towards the building. Only the weight of the bag acting as a counterbalance stopped her pitching headlong into the disgusting ooze. Louise was having no such difficulty shifting her load, despite having filled and moved three bags to each one of Alice's. She set the latest one down then came back and took Alice's.

'OK, I've decided to let you live. You can stop now.'

'It might be too late.'

'Don't die out here, that'll make me look heartless.' She opened the door and guided Alice into a big blue chair, then made her another coffee. 'Drink that and I'll go fetch lunch. Are you vegetarian or anything?'

Alice shook her head. Food? She could just sit still and Louise would bring her food? This must be how someone lost in the dessert feels when they reach an oasis. It seemed just a few minutes later when she heard a car horn beeping several times. She didn't have the strength to wonder why, much less get up and find out. It didn't matter. Louise, smelling of chips, was back to explain.

'That was what passes for a dinner bell round here.'

They were soon joined by the others and everyone was given a paper wrapped parcel as they came in. Alice opened hers to discover the most delicious battered fish and chips in the whole world ever.

She was hardly aware of Hamish, who'd perched on the arm of her chair, until a third of the way through her meal. When she did look up at him he seemed amused.

'No good asking if I can have some of your chips then?'

'Not a chance, pal.' She shielded them from view by folding over the paper.

'Louise and Alice obviously got on really well,' Nadeep said.

Alice hoped he wasn't thinking of taking up mind reading as a career.

'Yes, that's a truly impressive heap out there,' Hamish said.

Oh, got on with the rubbish clearing. Yes, they'd done that all right.

'You can't have stopped all morning,' he said.

'We didn't,' Louise admitted.

'It was too cold to stand around doing nothing,' Alice said. It wouldn't have been too cold to sit in the building, but to be fair she'd come to work.

As a reward for her efforts, Hamish said he'd take her into a hide for a closer look at the birds she'd been helping. The rest and the food had revived her and having Hamish for company restored her spirits. She was actually looking forward to seeing the birds, especially the one he'd helped rescue.

'Look what I've got,' she showed Hamish the microwaved sausage.

Everyone who was left in the staff building stared at it.

'Did you cut that off someone?' Louise asked.

It was then Alice realised it did look rather like an amputated body part. 'Well, he was annoying,' she said. 'I thought Snowball needed it more.'

'See!' Louise stuck her tongue out at Hamish. 'Told you Snowball was the best name for him. You should know better than to argue with a woman.'

'I'm learning,' Hamish said.

There was no sign of Snowball-Sausage so Alice left the snack where Hamish thought he'd be likely to find it. 'He's a lot less tame than he used to be and he doesn't know you, so he could be nearby keeping out of sight.'

'It's the wellies, isn't it?' Although the mud had worked its magic for a time, the long grass she and Louise walked through between it and the car park had restored them to their hideous brightness.

'Could be. Come on, let's get them out of sight.' He pushed open the door to the hide.

From the outside it looked like a garden shed. The inside, other than being clutter free and having a huge window, did little to alter the initial impression. There was a wooden bench to sit on and look out the window onto the water and yet more mud. A narrow shelf, presumably for people to rest their binoculars on, ran the length of the window. Nothing much seemed to be happening out there.

By the door a large blackboard stood ready for people to record their sightings. Yesterday's figures looked sparse, or perhaps there just hadn't been many non-feathered visitors to record the levels of the other kind? Huge charts on the walls meant Alice didn't have to admit she couldn't tell a tern from a gull.

'Gosh, I didn't know there were so many different types of sandpiper!' she said after studying it. She had realised a sandpiper was a bird, although she'd imagined them as tiny songbirds, not the lanky things depicted.

'We get all those here. We might be lucky today, but it's a bit early in the year.'

'Oh. I suppose that's why it says migrant? Sorry, I really don't know anything about birds.'

'No? What about those?'

She joined him on the bench and looked where he was pointing. 'Oyster catchers!'

They watched amused as the long legged birds seemed to race each other up and down over the silt. With their bright orange beaks constantly opening and closing they seemed to chatter amongst themselves.

'They're definitely planning something,' Alice decided.

'Like what?'

'Maybe they're going to fly in formation and impersonate a pterodactyl or something?'

'Now that's a murmuration I'd like to see,' Hamish said.

'A what? Oh it's the big flocks making patterns in the

evenings isn't it? Do oyster catchers do that? I thought it was just starlings.'

'Some other species do, but you're right it is mainly starlings. Have you seen them at Portsmouth harbour?'

'No.'

'I'll take you sometime, it's well worth seeing.'

'I'd like that. What are those?' Alice pointed to a group of birds, which although similar looking to the oyster catchers, were surely something else.

Hamish moved closer. 'The mostly white ones with upturned beaks?'

'Yes. I like them too.'

'They're avocets.'

Alice looked from one to the other. The avocets were altogether more delicate looking and had no red at all. Now Hamish had pointed out their beaks she could see it wasn't just that the avocet's were thinner and black which made them different. The shape was pretty weird. 'I think I'd recognise them again.'

'I'll test you next time. That's if you'd like to come again?'

'I would, yes. Oh, swans!'

'Two points to you.'

And two future dates arranged. Both involved bird watching. Was that a problem? No, she didn't think so, it was only because they were in a bird hide and she'd expressed an interest, not because he was forcing his hobby on her. She wondered if the Portsmouth starlings really were worth seeing. The murmurations she'd seen on *Springwatch* had been impressive, and from what she remembered that was just along the coast at Brighton. Obviously they only showed the best bits on TV, but Hamish could well be right about them being worth seeing and afterwards they'd be handily close to all the bars, clubs and restaurants at Gunwharf Quays.

Hamish put his arm around her and she snuggled up as close as she could. They stayed watching the birds, with Hamish explaining distinguishing features, as it grew dark. She didn't feel cold until Hamish stood up. It was as though he took her body heat with him and she started shivering.

'Alice, you're freezing. Sorry I hadn't realised.'

'I'm fine really, though I could do with something to warm me up.' She gave what she hoped was an encouraging smile.

'Hot chocolate back at mine?'

'Sounds like a plan.'

Hamish fetched a bag from his car on the way back to the staff building.

'I'll just get changed. Sorry, I didn't think to suggest you bring anything to change into. I carry spare clothes automatically.'

She looked down at her filthy clothes. 'I'm going to make an awful mess in your car.'

'Hmmm. My fault though. The coat's the worst. If you don't mind taking that off, I'll start the car so the heating gets going.'

He handed her a thick knitted sweater from his bag, turned the small fan heater towards her and switched it on full before going out. She bundled up her dad's coat so the mud was on the inside and put on the clothes she'd removed during her coffee break with Louise. On top of that she added his jumper. It was cosy and there was plenty of room. Anything of Tony's, had he allowed her to wear it, would have been a much snugger fit over her many layers.

Hamish returned, pulled off his boots, socks, sweater and jeans! She knew from her earlier experience there wasn't room to get undressed in the tiny bathroom and the kitchen was barely any bigger, so he really didn't have much option but to get changed in the same room as her. And he was a gorgeous, hunky fireman so she had no option but to watch.

She couldn't see much. His top half remained covered with a long sleeved polo shirt and although he'd removed one pair of socks he still wore another which came up to his knees, so really it was just his thighs. That wasn't too disappointing; those were some seriously muscular thighs! In moments they were covered again and he was ready to leave. Alice was feeling considerably warmer by then. She thawed further on the drive to his place. During the journey the car was filled with the pungent smell of river mud.

'A hot shower might be a good idea,' Hamish said once he'd parked the car.

'A very good idea,' Alice agreed. And if her overworked legs were too tired to hold her up and she needed someone with strong muscular thighs to lean on, whose fault would that be?

Hamish's narrow hallway contained a bicycle as well as a rack of coats and row of footwear. She added her boots, but not the filthy coat which they'd left spread over the back seat of Hamish's car to dry out. Hopefully the mud would then shake off. His flat was much like hers in terms of size and clutter, but a lot less brightly coloured and more open plan. It wasn't untidy exactly, but in the living area, piles of books, a remote controlled helicopter and various electronic gadgets topped the cupboards and coffee table. She liked it.

Hamish gently pulled her into his arms and she let her body slump against his as he held her. They stayed like that for a few moments, then he kissed her ear, her cheek, her lips. He kissed her until she was no longer aware of the ache in her legs, the pain in her arms and soreness of her back. All that mattered was his mouth on hers, his arms around her and that he never stop, never let go.

When he pulled away slightly his breathing was heavy and his voice low. 'Right, now let's get you out of these muddy clothes and properly warmed up.'

With his arm around her, he got her to the bathroom. When he let go to switch on the shower she sank down so she was sat on the toilet lid.

He chuckled and knelt down to remove her socks, all three pairs. 'Come on then, lift your arms,' he said when her feet were bare.

She obeyed and he stripped off layer after layer, throwing each in turn out into the hallway. It took a while as he kissed her again between every item of clothing.

## Chapter 12

When Hamish had removed everything but Alice's final T-shirt and jeans he stopped.

'You'd better see to the rest yourself or I won't be responsible for my actions.'

Irresponsible was just fine with her.

'And we won't get anything to eat and I definitely need something to eat.'

So did she, but her hunger for him was stronger.

'Pepperoni pizza with extra cheese?'

Ah, well maybe she could satisfy both appetites. It was still early and the food would give her more strength to enjoy what she hoped would follow.

'Yes please.'

'Right. Chuck your clothes outside the bathroom door and wear my dressing gown when you've finished.'

The water was the perfect temperature; almost too hot but not quite. It revived her sufficiently that she was able to wash her hair and body with Hamish's toiletries. It was a good thing she wasn't the kind of girl who worried about being seen without make-up, she thought as she dried herself, wrapped a towel round her head and put on Hamish's dressing gown. Anyway, even without mascara and lippy she probably looked better now than she had when she got into his car at the wildlife sanctuary. She felt better too; the hot water had eased her aching muscles and the tension in her back.

Alice's clothes were nowhere in sight and she could hear a washing machine whirring away. Oh good, she wouldn't be able to go home anytime soon.

Hamish got up as she walked into the living area. 'Feeling better?' he asked.

'Much, thank you.'

'Sorry, I don't have a hair dryer.'

'No problem.' She only used one when she was in a hurry and that wasn't the case just then. Tongs would have been good but she doubted her arms would have coped with holding them. She did think about combing her hair straight, got as far as finding her comb and decided that required too much effort.

Hamish settled her on the sofa, tucked a quilt around her and asked, 'Do you want the hot chocolate now, or later?' His grin and the sparkle in his eyes suggested he was asking about more than just the drink.

'Later I think.' That seemed to be the answer he'd wanted.

'Just going to have a shower myself. My wallet's here,' he placed it next to her comb on the coffee table, 'in case the pizza comes before I'm out, but it shouldn't do.'

'OK.' She wondered where he'd hidden all the stuff which had been on the table earlier. Under his bed perhaps? Hopefully she'd get to find out.

Hamish was back, clean, sweet smelling and changed before she'd imagined many of the details that might involve. He wore short legged and sleeved pyjamas, which meant more of his body was on display than she'd seen before. She liked what she saw; firm muscles, an even tan suggesting he spent a good part of the summer outside without excessive clothing, fair hairs on his chest and limbs, but not too much of it. Hamish, unlike Alice, was clearly unselfconscious about his body.

She was very, very conscious of his body. Especially the way those snug fitting shorts passed by at eye level and again when he returned with a bottle of wine and two glasses.

'Red OK?' He showed her the label.

'Perfect.'

He placed the glasses on the coffee table, pushed aside the end of the quilt and sat on the sofa next to her. Alice was conscious of the way her naked feet touched the warm skin of his thigh. Then, as he leant across to reach the bottle, of his weight on her.

Hamish poured a little wine into each glass and offered her one. She shuffled into a more upright position, accepted the drink and clinked her glass against his.

'Cheers.'

As they sipped the wine he hardly looked away from Alice. Not that she was noticing much. He leant across her again to swap his glass for her comb.

'Shall I?' He gestured with it.

'If you like.'

He gently combed through strands of her hair. She'd quite liked her mum doing that when she was little and enjoyed the hairdresser teasing her locks smooth, but this was a very different experience. It felt good to know Hamish's hands and attention were solely on her. It felt even better when he gently pulled her against him so he could do the side furthest from him. He was slow and gentle and thorough. Maybe he did everything that way. She really, really hoped so.

'What do you do with the front?' he asked. He crouched down in front of her, his cool grey-green eyes level with hers. His warm lips level with hers. Leaning closer he brushed damp tendrils off her face, stroking her hair smooth and caressing her cheeks with his thumbs. Then his lips brushed her forehead and she closed her eyes, tilting her head back a little. He nuzzled against her neck, then nipped her earlobe with his teeth.

The doorbell rang.

Hamish made a sound like a growl before giving her a quick kiss. He stood, turning away from her as he did. His walk to the door looked more awkward than the easy way he'd previously moved around the flat. Almost as awkward as the way he kept the lower part of his body behind the door as he opened it and paid the pizza delivery boy.

As well as an extra large pizza he'd ordered garlic bread, sour cream and chive dip and a tub of white chocolate ice cream. The pizza had a properly crisp base, rich tangy tomato sauce and plenty of slices of fiery hot pepperoni. The thick layer of gooey cheese pulled out into impressively long strands too. And the smell... possibly even better than the clean lemony scent clinging to Hamish's skin. The acidity of the dip was a perfect contrast to the buttery richness of the garlic bread.

The food wasn't better than having him kiss her, but it was an extremely nice way to fill in the time until he did it again. Hamish kept her wine glass topped up too. The ice cream, like the hot chocolate, was going to have to wait.

Once they'd finished eating, Hamish took the boxes away and returned with paper towels. He wiped her face and hands as though she were a candyfloss covered toddler. To show she was a grown woman, she stroked a towel over his cheek, then followed it with tiny kisses. She did the same on the other side and then to his mouth.

When he tried to return the kisses she murmured, 'I haven't finished yet,' and lifted one of his hands to her lips. She sucked clean each of his fingers in turn and was rewarded by hearing him groan again.

Hamish tugged at the quilt and wriggled under it with her.

'This is cosy,' Alice said. She turned and leant back against him, sighed as he slipped his arms around her, and relaxed.


When she woke the following morning, she was in Hamish's bed. He was sitting on the edge watching her, so she couldn't check underneath it for hastily tidied away clutter. That was the least of her disappointments. Not getting to the ice cream and hot chocolate were in second and third place. Having fallen asleep in his arms right after finishing her meal was way out in front though. He must have carried her to bed and she supposed they had slept together, but only in the most restful and innocent sense of the word.

'Morning,' Hamish said. 'I'm guessing you slept well?'

His bedside clock showed it was gone seven, so almost twelve hours since the pizza had been delivered.

'Must have, I don't remember a thing. Sorry.'

He shrugged. The grin he gave her suggested that although he might well be disappointed he wasn't annoyed.

'Tea or coffee?'

'Tea please.'

'While I make it you can decide what you want to do today.'

'What are my options?'

'I can drop you home in a minute, you can stay here, or come with me to the sanctuary.'

Staying where she was held the most appeal, or would have done if it wasn't for the fact she'd be alone. 'I'll come with you.'

'Great. Louise will be delighted.'

Good thing he was on his way out the room as he said that. Her expression couldn't possibly have been so cheerfully philosophical as his.

Over breakfast Alice checked her phone and saw that Kate had tried to call her the evening before. There was a text too, which read, 'Ring me when you've let that poor fireman off duty ;-)'

Alice texted back to say she'd be in touch in a day or two, if by then she had the strength to work her phone. Hopefully Kate would read it when she had a mouthful of orange juice and splutter it all over Pete, showing just how unladylike she was. She switched her phone off again afterwards, partly so it didn't go flat as she didn't have her charger with her and partly so she didn't have to deal with Kate's questions while Hamish was listening.

Almost everyone greeted Alice with as much warmth as on the previous day. The only exception was Louise; she was actually civil. The two women worked just as hard in just as much mud as previously, before going in for a tea break. When Alice stood to go back out she couldn't help but groan with discomfort.

'You OK?' Louise asked.

'Just a bit stiff.'

'Sorry, I've been rough on you. Stay here in the warm. There are magazines somewhere...'

'It's OK, I'll carry on... That's if you want me?'

'It's a lot easier with two.'

As they returned to the spot they were clearing Louise apologised for being rude before. 'I've seen Hamish hurt a few times by girls who throw themselves at him because he's gorgeous or because he's a fireman. They're only interested in the surface and it never lasts long.'

'It must be hard seeing that happen… to a friend.'

That was her second warning to take things steady. Kate had said she'd expected Alice to get tired of dating a fireman and get bored with Hamish. Perhaps she should listen? Not because she believed it was true, but because it just possibly could be. She'd fantasised over dating a fireman for so long that his job could blind her to his faults. She considered for a minute and couldn't think of a single one. Even when she'd been sure she loved Tony she'd seen clearly that he wasn't perfect. She didn't really know Hamish well enough to be in love, even if it did feel that way. And if Louise and Kate could see the possibility that her interest in Hamish was only uniform deep, surely Hamish himself would too.

The day involved five hours hard labour, a burger and apple pie lunch and a walk to inspect the handiwork of

Hamish and the others. As Louise pointed out various birds on the way, Alice warmed to her. Louise's enthusiasm was infectious and she managed to supply information without making Alice feel like an idiot for not knowing.

'Are you ready to go?' Hamish asked when they caught up with him.

'I should think the poor girl is ready to pass out,' Louise said. 'We've cleared all the rubbish right down to East Corner.'

'I'm all right,' Alice assured him. 'Nothing a shower and some food won't sort out.'

'We could try for the hot chocolate again,' he suggested as they walked towards his car.

She was very tempted, but if she went back to his place, and managed to stay awake her behaviour was definitely going to come into the throwing herself at him category. Besides her toothbrush and other things she was going to need before work on Monday were all in her flat.

'Another time. I really should go back to mine if you don't mind driving me there.'

'Sure. No problem.'

Alice hardly noticed the drive back to her flat. She jolted into awareness as he stopped the car.

'So... can I see you again?' Hamish asked. He actually looked as though he expected her to say no.

Clearly she'd overdone the backing off. 'Yes. Yes, of course. Let's have dinner tonight. I'll pay.' Oh god, that sounded desperate. Why couldn't she manage to say something which was 'keen but not total slut'?

'Yes to dinner, no to you paying.'

'But...' She didn't have the strength to argue, it could wait until she'd recovered a bit.

'Pick you up at seven then?' Hamish said.

Alice spent ages scrubbing off the mud and conditioning her hair, but didn't bother applying much make-up. If how she'd looked when she and Louise staggered back to the staff building hadn't put him off then Hamish wasn't going to be bothered by a lack of blusher. She did choose a figure hugging jersey dress and high heeled boots though. Just because she wasn't going to throw herself at him didn't mean he had to want her to keep her distance.

She was ready at a quarter to seven and gave Kate a call.

'You out with Hamish tonight... or staying in with him?'

'Out tonight, in last night. All night.'

'Oh! No wonder you didn't answer your phone! I wouldn't have rung if I thought I might be interrupting something.'

'Actually you'd have woken me up.' She explained about working at the sanctuary and falling asleep.

'Oh, disappointing. Did you make up for it this morning?'

'No. We went back to the sanctuary and I spent the day mud wrestling with Louise.'

'That doesn't sound much fun.'

'That bit wasn't fun exactly, but it's a useful thing to do, I'm sure I'll feel good about it once I stop aching. Watching the birds was quite interesting.'

'Be careful, Sis. You went along with the dull stuff Tony liked and said that was educational, you don't want to fall into the same trap.'

'I won't, but if he's really interested I'm going to have to accept it, aren't I? Just as I'll expect him to accept the things I want to do. I'll give it a go, if I'm still interested once the novelty has worn off I'll carry on and it'll be something we can share. If I don't, well I'll just have to find a hobby of my own.'

'Dad has some wine bottles going spare.'

'OK, you've convinced me – I'm off to buy binoculars and a notebook.'

'Hey, how did that work?' Kate asked.

'Dunno, but I'd better go and finish getting ready, Hamish will be here soon.'

'OK, have fun.'

Alice applied another coat of lash-building mascara, lined her lips in cherry red, filled them in with her glossiest lippy, and gave herself a good spritz of scent. That was better, she felt like Alice again, not like a forest ranger who happened to scrub up OK.

When Hamish called, he hugged and kissed her but released her quickly and kept his hands to himself. His eyes though, she noticed, were doing their best to make up for him not using his sense of touch to discover exactly how the soft wool of her dress clung to, and accentuated, every curve.

'So where would you like to go?' he asked.

'Somewhere close which serves huge portions. I'm starved.'

At the Sunken Yacht, Alice ordered fish with extra chips. 'They're for you, I'm going to eat every one of mine.' She did, followed by sticky toffee pudding and custard. She turned down the offer of alcohol though and opted for Coke in the hope of staying awake.

When the waitress asked if they'd like more coffee she declined; she'd want to sleep eventually. 'Just the bill please,' she said.

'It's already been paid.'

How had he managed that? 'Thanks, but you don't always have to pay.'

'I didn't have to, I just did.' He winked, then reached over and took her hand. 'Thank you for your efforts at the sanctuary.'

Nadeep had already thanked her profusely and even Louise had expressed a certain amount of gratitude. Hamish though probably guessed that her efforts had been for his benefit.

'No problem. It's been an interesting couple of days.'

'Have you enjoyed this weekend, Alice?'

It wasn't over yet... was it? Perhaps it had to be. She wouldn't be any better at controlling her desires if they went back to her place than if she'd gone home with him. If her short term options were limited at least she could try to ensure she had some long term ones.

'I can't say I'm a fan of the mud, but it was good to do something more useful than shopping or watching TV and I do like the birds. They're fascinating when you really look.'

'Yeah? So you want to see the murmurations?'

'Definitely.'

'Then how about I pick you up after work on Tuesday or

Wednesday? I wouldn't be able to stay out late, but we'd have time to see them if we went straight there and could grab something to eat on the way back.'

'Tell you what, take me to see them and I'll cook you something afterwards.' At least he wouldn't be able to pay for that, not with cash anyway. Hopefully he'd do so another way eventually – and by then she'd be owed some interest.

'Deal'. Hamish gave a big grin. 'And, er, no pressure or anything, but at the end of the month I'm going to Wales birdwatching for a few days. I'm staying in a cottage in the middle of nowhere. Want to keep me company?'

Alice liked the idea very much. That gave her a couple more weeks to find out if she really liked him personally and not because he fit her fantasy so well. And if it seemed they really were keen on each other, then being somewhere remote with nothing to distract them during the long evenings could be very good indeed.

'I'm owed lots of time off and things are quiet at work so it shouldn't be a problem.' Miles would probably try to make it difficult, but since splitting with Tony she was more confident and wasn't going to let him mistreat her.

Hamish almost had to carry her back to her place so he probably wasn't surprised not to be invited in. Alice was too tired to notice if he looked disappointed.


She overslept the next morning and missed her bus. When she stepped off the next one she ran all the way to work and got in at ten past nine. Kath was just ending a telephone call.

'Fire alarm went off again. I'd better tell Miles.'

While she was gone Alice learned the fire brigade had

received two hoax calls to the premises over the weekend.

'Do you mean the automatic system is going off when it shouldn't, or that someone is actually phoning the fire brigade?' Alice asked.

'Both I think,' Lucy said. 'Miles was ranting about the IT people saying they'd buggered up the system and about kids wasting everyone's time. Apparently he gets called out whenever there's a problem, so he had to come in three times over the weekend.'

'His mood is going to be worse than usual then,' Alice said.

When Kath returned she said, 'Miles wants a word at ten.'

She should just have stayed in bed. He was either going to reprimand her for being late or was connecting her to the hoax calls. There wasn't much she could say in her defence about either of those but she could see that from Miles's point of view both problems could be solved by giving her the sack. Great, just as one area of her life was starting to look promising, another was about to fall apart.

## Chapter 13

Alice soon realised she'd made a mistake and it wasn't just her Miles wanted to talk to. There was to be a meeting with all staff down in the warehouse. The general opinion was that Tatisuz was to either close down or be sold.

'We'll get redundancy, won't we?' Emma asked.

'Yes, but not much,' Kath said. 'It'll be less than one pay cheque.'

'That can't be right. My dad got thousands. A couple of years' pay at least and that was compulsory redundancy.'

'Sorry,' Kath said, 'but I've looked into it. The legal minimum is one week's wages for every complete year we've worked here and I can't see Miles having paid into any scheme or insurance or anything so we get more, can you?'

Alice looked round at her colleagues' miserable faces. Much as Miles annoyed her and the job bored her, she didn't want to lose it before she'd found something better. She mentally kicked herself for not having already tried to do that. She hadn't thought the problems with Tatisuz were quite so serious and there didn't seem to be many job opportunities about. Kath, who had children, must have been really concerned though, if she'd taken the trouble to find out their legal position.

'What are we going to do?' Emma's question was probably in everyone's mind.

Alice knew her parents would let her move back in with them if she couldn't keep up her rent. Lucy still lived with hers. They were the lucky ones though. Things would be harder for the other women and presumably for most of the men too.

'Maybe it won't be as bad as that?' Alice suggested. 'If he's got a buyer then we might keep our jobs.' She didn't suppose they all would, the new boss would probably want to make changes but it might give them a bit of breathing space.

'Let's get ourselves a drink and go down,' Kath said. 'If he sees we're ready, maybe he'll get it over with.'

Down in the warehouse the men were huddled together, looking just as glum as their office colleagues.

'Do you know what he wants to talk to us about?' one of the forklift truck drivers asked.

'No, but...'

Kath stopped when the driver interrupted with, 'He's here.'

Miles must have realised the women had all gone down to the unusually quiet warehouse, and followed them.

'I didn't realise you'd all be so eager for a chat,' he said.

He was the only one who even attempted to laugh at his feeble joke. Even by Miles's standards, treating this as funny was rotten behaviour.

'Is everyone here?' Miles asked.

'Except for Dave. He's off sick.'

'Really? I didn't realise City were playing today.'

Some of the men shuffled uncomfortably, convincing Alice that Miles was right to be sceptical. What was he planning to do; blame the company's failure on inefficient staff?

'There's no need to pass on any of what I'm going to say to

him, I'll speak to him separately when he comes back.'

If whatever he had to say didn't apply to Dave perhaps they weren't all going to be sacked?

Miles said, 'I'll get on with it then. Firstly, thank you all for bearing with me during the last few difficult months. I'm sure you've realised that business had slowed down and that I've been unable to invest in the company as I'd have liked.'

Things had been 'difficult' at work for over a year and Alice couldn't remember Miles ever spending a penny he wasn't pretty much forced to, unless it was on himself, but she nodded along with the rest.

'That's about to change. I've negotiated a big contract which will begin in the new financial year. Until then, money will still be tight, but once in effect I will be in a position to consider personnel matters and make improvements to our infrastructure. I'd like your help in identifying the actions which will be most advantageous to my workforce.'

'Does all this mean we'll get a pay rise?' Kath asked.

'Eventually, yes. Stay with me and your loyalty will be rewarded.'

It seemed like a long time before anyone spoke.

'So you're not closing the company down?' Kath asked.

'No of course not. Why would you think that?' He seemed so surprised that Alice thought maybe he hadn't deliberately let them jump to the wrong conclusion about the reason for the meeting.

Miles continued, with some heat, 'I've built this company up from nothing and invested a great deal of time and money into it. I have no intention of letting that all go to waste.' He took a breath. 'And all of you have put your time into the company too. We all want it to succeed, don't we?'

There were many assurances of that.

'Excellent. Then let's get ready for the next phase. I want a stocktake so we know exactly what we've got. Kath and Lucy, perhaps you could deal with the paperwork side of that? Alice and Emma, I want a real sales push. Get onto all our customers and say there's a ten per cent discount for all orders paid for in full by the end of this month.'

Everyone got to work immediately. Alice didn't even stop to text Kate, to say she had good news, until her official lunch break.

'I'll pick you up from work. Tell me then or now?' Kate texted back.

'Later. Something else to talk about too.'

'Me too.'

'???'

'Laterz!!!'

'So what's the good news?' Kate asked as soon as Alice got into her car.

'Miles has got some big new orders and we're all getting pay rises.'

'Oh! That is good news.'

'I know. When he said he wanted to speak to us all we thought we were all going to get the sack.' She explained about the meeting.

'Did he say how much of a rise, or when?'

'Well no, but I suppose he's got to wait until the orders are processed so he can work it out. He only had it confirmed just before he told us.'

'Ah, right. And the other thing you wanted to talk about?'

'No, your turn. More good news, I hope?'

'Yes, well I think so. I've decided to move in with Pete.'

'It's good, but it's not exactly news. You've been gradually doing that since just after Christmas.'

'Well you know me, I don't like to rush into anything.'

'You've been together quite a while.'

'Not as long as you and Tony were.'

'True, but Pete's nothing like Tony. You knew he was no good for me and I should have listened. I can see Pete is good for you, are you going to listen to me?'

'Absolutely, especially the bit where you explain it to Mum and Dad.'

'Kate, you've been moving in over the last ten weeks, I think they'll have noticed by now... but since you want me to tell them I'll do a big announcement and get Dad to crack open a bottle of wine to celebrate.' Fortunately they'd arrived outside Alice's flat by then so she was able to jump out and make a run for it, leaving Kate to park before she could follow.

'Good idea of yours,' she said as she came in. 'I've phoned Dad and told him to put a bottle in the fridge... and that I'll be driving you over and back so I can't have any.'

'That's just mean!'

'Yes, I know.' Kate adopted a smug expression.

'Tea?'

'Yes please.'

'Arsenic or strychnine?'

Kate blew her a kiss. 'OK, no wine, and you're right I'll just tell them, not make a big fuss about it.'

'You've already told them! Is there something you're not telling me? There's something wrong with Pete? Or... Mum or Dad are ill?'

'No!'

'What then?'

'It doesn't seem right for me to be so happy when you're not.'

Alice had to swallow several times to shift the lump in her throat. 'Oh, Kate. Look, I'm absolutely fine and even if I wasn't, seeing you all loved up would make me feel better not worse.'

They hugged.

'Now, what was your other thing?' Kate asked.

'A couple of things, actually. There have been more hoax calls to the fire brigade and there's nothing other than me connecting where I live to where I work. Do you think someone has got it in for me?'

'What? God, Tony really got you paranoid, didn't he? Oh, you think it might be him?'

'The thought has crossed my mind. He was pretty upset and he's not keen on firemen.'

'He's not an idiot either though, is he? I can't see it somehow.'

That was a relief to Alice; she hadn't wanted to believe it.

'Have you spoken to Hamish about it?'

'No, I haven't.'

'He'd know more about this sort of thing than we would.'

'True, but I don't want to make a big thing about him being a fireman.'

'Eh? I'm pretty sure the guy knows what he does for a living. Those engines and the flames and stuff would be hard to miss and anyway, I thought the big thing about him is that he is a fireman?'

'No! It isn't. Arrrgh. If I can't make you see that, what chance have I got with him?'

'Make my own tea, shall I?' Kate said. She poured the boiling water onto the tea bags Alice had already put into mugs.

'You said you thought I'd get fed up with him once the novelty of him being a fireman wore off.'

'I thought it might. I take it that hasn't happened then?'

'No. I like him a lot.'

'Like?' Kate asked.

'Yes. OK, I am totally in lust too, obviously, but I do like him and not because of his uniform or anything.'

'OK.'

Alice narrowed her eyes at Kate.

Kate raised her hands in surrender. 'I believe you, Sis. OK?'

'OK, but I don't know how to convince him. Remember I told you about his friend Louise...?'

'The slave driver at the sanctuary? Oooh that sounds like a

scary film. Well anyway, what about her?'

'She said women were always throwing themselves at Hamish just because he's a fireman.'

'She's probably just jealous. From what you said I reckon she'd like to do the same, but is so bony she'd just bounce off.'

Alice, grinning at the image, wondered just how much she confided in Kate without realising she did it. 'Maybe, I'm not totally sure, but I think she's right about this. Actually, I know she is. When we go out together women are always trying to talk to him and touch his arm and things. Can you imagine what it's like when he's on his own or just with his mates and in uniform?'

'Hmm, yes. I've been out with good looking guys, not that Pete is hideous or anything, but some people attract attention and your Hamish is definitely one of them.'

'Exactly. And Louise said he's got hurt before, thinking girls are serious and then finding out any hunky fireman would do. I don't want him thinking I'm another one of those, which he probably does because he knows I've got a thing about them.'

'So you want to show you're serious? Ah, so that's what all the up to your elbows in mud was about?'

'Yes. Well, a bit to start with, but I did like watching the birds and I liked helping them... well, knowing I was helping, not so much the actual work.' She told Kate about the suggested trip to Wales and her intention of not 'throwing herself' at Hamish until then.

'You mean you haven't...?'

'No. We will, but I want to wait a bit, if I can.'

'The bird stuff should help. With Louise around you won't be able to get up to anything. And how about inviting him to a family dinner? Me and Pete are doing one next Sunday; I thought if I invited Mum and Dad they'd see I wasn't abandoning them any more than you did when you came here.'

'D'you think they're wishing we'd just leave them alone?'

'Nah. They'd hide the cakes in that case.'


Hamish rang on Tuesday morning to arrange to take her round to Portsmouth to see the murmurations on Wednesday evening.

'That's fine. Anything in particular you'd like me to cook for you?'

'Would you mind if we ate out and did that another night? William is having car trouble and he doesn't want to leave his wife without hers. Jeff's picking him up tonight, but as I'll be coming past his place on the way back to yours, it makes sense for me to do it tomorrow.'

'OK. That's fine.'

The murmurations were indeed spectacular. Easily as good as the versions she'd seen on TV. Better actually as she could appreciate the scale.

'I can't believe I didn't know about this.' She loved spotting smaller groups gather in the distance and then join up with the main flock. Surely they must communicate with each other somehow to be able to do that without any mid-air collisions?

Even more amazing was to watch birds breakaway from

the main group and head, at high speed, for their roosts under the railway station. Sometimes they'd seem to lose their nerve and veer away at the last moment, but not once did they crash into the supports.

The Thai curry afterwards was something of a disappointment. Far too sweet and glutinous. It was almost a good thing they didn't have time to savour it. With William in the car and Red Watch about to go on duty Hamish didn't have long to linger over kissing her goodnight either.

Alice's next date with Hamish was another game of bowling with his friends from Red Watch. At least this time he warned her in advance. She decided a casual look would be best, something warm, comfortable and which wouldn't be too distracting for Jeff. Would her jeans be too tight? She pulled them on and discovered they weren't tight at all! The bathroom scales confirmed she really had lost weight and not just forgotten how well her clothes fitted. That had to be down to the work at Beaulieu wildlife sanctuary.

Again the bowling evening was fun. William brought the image of his wife Sandra's latest ultrasound scan to show her. Although Alice wasn't overly fascinated by the blurry black and white picture of the developing baby, it was sweet how excited William was at the prospect of becoming a father.

'His wife begs us to take him out to give her a break from him going on about it and sitting with his hands on her so he can feel it kick,' Jeff said.

'You're just jealous,' William said.

'Nah, I get my hands on your missus all the time.'

William just shook his head. It was clear he didn't believe a word of it. Nor did Alice. She thought it far more likely William was right and that Jeff would like to be in a similar position. She guessed Jeff's over the top humour and inappropriate comments were a cover for his insecurity when it came to women and that if he were to meet the right girl he'd be better behaved.

Almost as though he could read her thoughts, Jeff said, 'How's your sister?'

'She's fine, but I'm not introducing you.'

'Aww, why not?'

'I like her.'

Jeff pretended to sulk, sticking his bottom lip right out as Hamish and William laughed.

'That reminds me, Hamish,' she said when Jeff got up to take his turn. 'Kate has invited us to lunch on Sunday, with our parents. You're working though, aren't you?'

'I am, but on lates, so I could make it if you don't mind me eating and running.'

'No, that's fine.'

'I've got an invitation for you too, actually.'

'Oh?'

'From Louise. She said if you wanted to join her any weekend she'd be delighted to work you mercilessly until you passed out face down in the mud. She said something about being sure she could pass it off as an accident?'

Alice grinned but didn't explain. She had no intention of saying anything which might suggest she and one of his oldest friends hadn't hit it off straight away. Being friends with Louise might be a good move and the work which would be involved offered benefits too, including filling her time whilst Hamish was at work. Sometimes she'd hear a siren and worry he was on the way to a dangerous situation.

At the end of the evening, Hamish again gave Jeff and William a lift home, so she had no choice but to contain her sexual desires. Her plan had been to raise the subject of the hoax calls when he walked her to her door, but they'd only got as far as agreeing that he'd pick her up at twelve on Sunday, to go over to Kate's, by the time they got there. Further conversation would have taken up valuable kissing time, so she kept quiet except for a moan of pleasure as he held her tight and let her feel that he wanted her as much as she wanted him.

On the drive to Kate's, Alice told Hamish about the hoax calls to work. 'Maybe I'm being paranoid, but after the one at the flat I can't help thinking they're connected to me in some way.'

'There haven't been any more to the flats.'

'No, I don't think so. Oh...' He'd been telling her, not asking her. She should have realised he'd know. He must know about the ones to Tatisuz too and probably wondered why she hadn't told him. 'Do you think they're connected?'

'I doubt it. You don't like your boss much, do you?'

'No.' Where was this going?

'Is it personal, or do other staff feel that way?'

'No one likes him, well they didn't anyway. You think someone has got it in for him? Yes, that's much more likely!' Gosh she had got herself into a state over it; of course it was more likely that a disgruntled employee of Miles's was responsible. 'Perhaps it's all over now then?' She gave him a brief summary of the staff meeting.

'Let's hope so.'

Alice thought about telling him that she'd spent a few hours at the wildlife sanctuary the previous day, but decided not to. He'd probably find out from Louise, but if he didn't that wouldn't matter. Surprisingly, Alice realised she intended to carry on giving up some of her time and it wasn't just to win his approval.

She'd got the bus over, taking spare clothes with her. It was clear that Louise hadn't expected her to show up. Alice couldn't tell for sure whether she was pleased or not to have had her challenge accepted. Having no intention of being pushed to exhaustion again she'd made it clear she could only stay for two hours.

'Is there anything useful I can do in that time?' she'd asked.

'More rubbish clearing, if you're up for it?'

'Absolutely.' She couldn't hide her dismay though when they went to exactly the same area they'd worked in before and she saw a fresh load of litter waiting to be collected.

'It's an ongoing job,' Louise said. 'More gets brought in on the tide every day.'

'We'd best get started then.'

Alice had worked as hard as she could for two hours.

'Got time for a coffee before you have to get going?' Louise asked at the end of the time.

'That'd be great.'

Louise made the coffee as Alice got changed, and chatted quite pleasantly as they drank it. She wrote her number out and gave it to Alice. 'It's fine to just turn up and help. As you've seen there's always rubbish to clear, but if you let me know in advance maybe I can find you something more interesting to do another time.'

'Huh! You just want me up a tree or something so you can give me a shove.'

'Damn! Didn't think you'd cotton on to that.'

Alice left with a grin on her face. She'd worked hard, done something useful and seemed to be on the way to making a new friend. And surely she'd already burned off the calories she'd eat at Kate's?

The meal was a success, despite the accompanying carrot wine. Her dad's vinification 'skills' were something else Alice hadn't told Hamish about. Fortunately for him he'd refused any alcohol due to having to drive and then going onto a late shift. He probably learned all he needed from everyone else's expressions as they drank theirs though.

Alice allowed herself a moment's fantasy of presenting Louise with a bottle for helping to teach her about conservation work. Tempting, but the poor woman didn't deserve that; all she'd done was threaten murder. She felt a laugh trying to escape and looked around at Kate for help. Mistake. Kate held up the vegetable dish, containing carrots, broccoli and parsnips. 'Would you like some sprouts?' she asked.

The pair of them dissolved into the same uncontrollable giggles that vegetable had created during the Christmas dinner.

'You're a brave man, son,' Alice's dad said to Pete.

Her mum asked, 'Do you have any brothers or sisters, Hamish?'

'I do, a brother called Donald.'

'Oh another Scottish name. Are your family from Scotland?'

'Yes, originally. I have a few cousins there and actually that's where Donald is working at the moment, but we and my parents were born in England.'

Alice was puzzled for a moment. These were the kind of questions her mum asked people she didn't know very well... but of course her parents hadn't met Hamish before. It hadn't felt like that.

The next time they went out, Hamish took her to see a romantic comedy. During the kissing and slightly erotic scenes she glanced at him. Each time he was looking at her with a hunger she doubted popcorn would satisfy.

Tempting as it was to answer his query about what she'd like to do next with, 'go back to my place and act out what we've just seen,' she restrained herself.

'Let's call in at the Sunken Yacht for a drink and I absolutely insist on paying this time.'

'If you absolutely insist, I suppose I have no choice.'

She bought the drinks and placed them next to a sheet of paper. On it was written a telephone number she recognised.

'It's where the hoax call to your flat came from.'

'Oh!' Alice stared at the familiar number.

Hamish squeezed her hand. 'You recognise it, don't you?'

## Chapter 14

'Yes. It's Tony's number.' That's what she'd feared, but these continued hoaxes didn't seem like something he'd do. He got angry sometimes but always calmed down quickly and he wasn't reckless. 'Why would he do this?'

'You know him better than me, but he seemed a bit unbalanced when I met him.'

'Because he was so jealous.'

'Particularly of firemen?'

'Yes. It's a family joke about me and firemen and Kate teased him about it.'

'Tony doesn't do jokes, I take it?'

'He used to...' It was horrible to think she'd upset him so much he was risking people's lives and getting himself into trouble.

Hamish did his best to reassure her. 'This is in no way your fault. Someone will speak to him, in fact they'll have done it already, explaining why hoax calls are so dangerous and what the penalties might be. Unless he's completely stupid, he'll stop.'

'You're right, he'll have seen sense by now. Thanks.' She needed to change the subject. 'Now... this cottage in Wales. Does it have electricity?'

'It does. No TV or phone signal though. We'll have to make our own entertainment.'

His grin told her exactly what kind of fun he had in mind. When he accepted her invitation to come in for coffee, she hoped to get a practical demonstration.

He pulled her into his arms and kissed her fiercely before she could think of filling the kettle. He slid a warm hand inside her sweater and over her bare skin. Her back arched under his touch and she moaned with pleasure. Alice couldn't seem to control her own hands. They wanted to stroke his face, push through his hair and rake her nails down his back.

The kisses went on and on, becoming slower and more gentle as Alice's heart pounded and her breathing became frantic. Not just her breathing. She wanted him so much. She had him there in her arms, his weight on her. Alice screamed joyfully, then went limp.

Gradually her breathing and pulse slowed to normal and she realised they were lying fully clothed just inside her front door.

'I can see Wales is going to be very entertaining indeed.' Hamish pulled her to her feet. 'Now, do I get that coffee or did you get me up here under false pretences?'

He did get a mug of coffee but that was all. It seemed he too had decided to wait until they got to Wales before taking things any further.


Kath left the office and went to the bank during her lunch break. She returned with a huge bouquet of lilies and roses which she presented to Alice. 'I was asked to give you these. Chap who brought them is waiting outside.'

'He's not six foot with really blond hair, is he?' Alice asked.

'No. Dark haired. Actually I think it's your ex, looks like

the bloke you brought to the Christmas party.'

'I was afraid of that.'

She'd have ignored him, but Miles returned from his own break and said, 'Did you know your ex-boyfriend is waiting outside?'

'Yes. Sorry if he's being a nuisance, Miles.'

'It's not your fault. Shall I come down with you and see he doesn't do anything daft?'

Thinking that would be the quickest way to get rid of Tony she agreed.

'Alice, get in the car so we can talk privately,' Tony said as she approached.

She didn't need Miles muttering in her ear to know that probably wasn't a good idea. 'Just say whatever it is you've come to say, Tony, and go.'

'I love you, Alice. Give me another chance.'

'No, Tony.' She spoke gently. 'It's over. It would be best for you to accept that and not contact me again... or the fire brigade.'

He seemed to shrink. 'You know? I'm sorry, Alice. That was a really stupid thing to do. I was so angry when I saw you with that fireman and I'd been drinking... but it's no excuse.'

'It certainly isn't,' Miles snapped. 'Now stop harassing my employee.' He put a hand on Alice's shoulder and steered her away.

'Alice, please!' Tony called.

She didn't look back.

'Are you OK?' Miles asked.

'I'm fine. Thank you.' She'd have liked to get back to work and try to forget it, but he took her into his office and made tea.

'Do the police know it was him making the hoax calls?' Miles asked.

'I'm not sure, but the fire brigade do and they'll take action.'

'Do you think he's dangerous? Would he start a fire?'

'No, I'm sure he wouldn't.' She was sure; almost.

'It's worrying, especially with him hanging around here at night.'

Alice jerked her head up.

'I didn't realise who it was of course, but twice I've come by after a night out and seen his Audi.'


Miles called another staff meeting that afternoon. He told everyone they weren't to worry as he was going to have CCTV installed and arrange fire training. No one had been particularly worried before, but they started speculating furiously afterwards. Learning how to use extinguishers and listening to talks on fire safety were a novelty though and broke up the tedious working days a bit. The promised increase in business wasn't yet having any impact.

Miles gave each member of staff a key and requested that, if they were in the area outside of working hours, they drove down the track to check everything was OK. 'Don't get out your car though, I don't want anyone to take risks on my behalf.'

'Yeah, right,' Kath muttered. 'Like I'm going to come into

work after hours.' It seemed to be a common sentiment.

Hamish came round for spaghetti bolognese that evening. She hadn't cooked what used to be her signature dish for ages as Tony turned his nose up the first time she'd made it for him. Apparently she would have needed streaky bacon, rosemary and celery to be authentic.

'This is really great,' Hamish said as he finished a second portion. 'I've never had it with chilli in before.'

'I tried it once when I'd run out of black pepper and liked it.'

'Genius!'

That word being how she often referred to her mum's truly exceptional cooking made the compliment all the better.

When Hamish helped wash up in her tiny kitchen and spotted the fresh herbs on her windowsill he was even more impressed. So was she. Tony loaded the dishwasher at his place, but she'd never seen him with his hands in a sink of greasy water except the once after Christmas dinner and there he'd had a sizeable audience to impress. She wasn't going to spoil the time she had with Hamish before he went in for a night shift by thinking about Tony, though.

Instead they talked. She learned William's wife was expecting a daughter and Jeff had a girlfriend.

'She seems sane, so I doubt it'll last.'

'He can't be that bad or you wouldn't be friends with him,' Alice pointed out.

'He's fun, but not exactly politically correct, is he?'

'True. I don't think that's the real problem. Seems to me he's putting on a front of not caring much, but underneath he'd happily be in William's situation.'

'You noticed that too? So what advice can I give him?'

'About not scaring women away? Treat them with respect. Real respect, not all this getting upset over words like chairman and insisting on chairperson, just treat them like people with opinions and personalities not with hidden agendas and guilty secrets.'

'OK, I'll see Jeff takes note.'

Ah. Not just Jeff. Still, to be fair she hadn't just been thinking of him either.

Hamish gave a cheeky wink when she'd offered coffee.

'Just coffee?'

'Ah all right, I'll let you have some of my After Eights.'

She was only half glad he didn't suggest anything more exciting, but knew she was doing the right thing by getting to know him first. It was a good thing too that she was spending time with her family and having nights out with friends she'd reconnected with at the school reunion. The trips to the wildlife sanctuary looked set to become a regular thing too. Louise hadn't suddenly become her best friend but she greeted Alice at least as warmly as the spray-tanned scrap of skin and muscle who worked on reception at the gym she and Tony had used. Sausage-Snowball had put in an appearance on one occasion which pleased Alice enormously. Besides, wading through mud was more beneficial all round than battling with shiny fitness machines. She wanted Hamish so, so much, but she wasn't going to allow herself to become reliant on one person for her entire social life ever again.

A paramedic on a motorbike roared down the track to where Alice worked. Medical kit in hand, he ran into the building.

'Where is she?' he demanded of those staff who'd rushed out from the warehouse and down from the offices to see what was wrong.

'There's no problem here. It must be another hoax,' Miles informed him.

Before he'd convinced the paramedic of that an ambulance and fire engine arrived. Alice recognised the fire crew as people from Red Watch, but Hamish, William and Jeff weren't among them.

'We had a call saying someone was trapped under fallen shelving,' the paramedic explained.

Most of the storage area was visible from the entranceway, but Miles invited him and other members of the emergency services to look while he ensured all staff were accounted for. Miles explained about the hoaxes. 'I've been told they were made from pay phones, making it impossible to trace who made them.'

The paramedic went to confer with the ambulance driver, then said, 'Not an anonymous hoax this time. The caller was a Miles Molde. They're trying to contact him now to see if we have the wrong address, but I don't think that's very likely.'

'That's me. I'm Miles Molde, but I've been here all morning.' He looked round at his staff who nodded in agreement.

'Does the name Alice Bakewell mean anything to you?' the paramedic asked.

'I didn't. I wouldn't,' Alice said.

'That's the name we were given for the victim. '

Alice shuddered. Being trapped under fallen wood and metal sounded very much like the accident she'd had as a child with her dog Frodo. She couldn't remember ever telling Tony about it, but it was likely that she had. Plenty of people did know, including everyone she'd gone to school with. Rachel would definitely have known. Whoever was doing this was clearly targeting her. Why would anyone want to hurt her? Louise did; she'd said she'd drown her. Alice's ears pounded as though her head were under water and she felt weak from lack of air. She was so, so cold.

Miles caught her as she sank to her knees. 'I'd better take you home.'

'No!' Whoever was doing this knew where she lived. 'To my parents.' Her enemy might know their address too, but at least she wouldn't be alone there.

'Come on then, lean on me.' Miles helped her into his car and made sure she was buckled in safely. 'Coleville Avenue, isn't it?'

'Yes. Thank you.'

Alice's mum wrapped her in a crocheted blanket, gave her hot water bottles, sweet tea and cake. By the time her dad finished work and Kate called in, on her way home from her job at the bank, Alice was feeling silly for reacting so badly. Obviously someone was deliberately causing trouble and it must be someone who knew her, but that didn't mean they intended to kill her. Louise had said that; surely she wouldn't if she'd actually meant it and anyway, the hoaxes had started before the two women met. No, Louise just resented her relationship with Hamish, or was warning her not to hurt him or something. She wouldn't involve the fire brigade in that.

Rachel seemed too cold and rational to make hoax calls, even if she was secretly in love with Tony. And if that were the case she'd have stopped, not started after Alice broke up with him. And Tony himself? He seemed the obvious suspect and she knew he'd made at least one call, but she still couldn't believe he'd go to these lengths. That suggested desperation. Tony had been upset at the split and his pride was hurt, but she was sure he'd never been desperately in love with her. It had to be him though, didn't it? Perhaps he'd had some kind of breakdown or something.

'Sorry I got in such a state,' she said to her family. 'I got the silly idea someone was threatening what would actually happen to me and it reminded me of being trapped with Frodo.'

'You're not silly, love. You come home for a while.'

'There's no need, Mum.' She loved her parents but they tended to smother their 'baby' daughter.

'Sorry, I think Mum's right to be worried,' Kate said. 'This isn't just Tony being annoyed you dumped him. It's more than that.'

'Tony wouldn't be so stupid,' her dad said. 'He always was a bit odd, but not dangerous, surely?'

'No,' Alice said. 'Once when we had a row while he was driving he pulled over and stopped to cool down because he wasn't safe to drive and might hurt someone.'

'Talking of cars, if you must go, you'll take mine,' her mum said. 'You're insured and I never use it.'

'Yes you do, Mum. You use it for work, shopping and

going down the library.'

'I'll get the bus. You're not to. I don't want you going out anywhere on your own and you're to drive to work. Promise me?'

'OK. Thanks. Actually maybe I will stay here, just until I go to Wales.' That was only two days; she could survive being fussed over and force-fed cake for that long. She'd be sleeping in Kate's room so it wasn't as though she was regressing to childhood.

Miles called to ask how she was.

'I'm fine now, thank you.'

'That's good, but obviously it was a horrible shock. You needn't come in to work until after your holiday if you don't feel up to it.'

'Thank you. I...' She nearly said she was fine again, but knew if she went in to work the others would keep talking about the incident and the other hoaxes, plus it was daft to turn down a couple of free days off when they were offered. 'That's nice of you, Miles. It might be better not to be reminded just yet.'

'Alice... the police have been in contact and would like a statement. I said having them turn up at your parents' home this afternoon might be upsetting and I'd let you know.'

'Thank you. That was thoughtful.'

He gave her the details of how to contact the police and who to ask for, then added, 'Have a nice time, wherever it is you're going.'

'I will, thank you.' She was glad she hadn't told anyone, other than Kate and her parents, where exactly she was spending her week off.

Alice's mum drove her to the police station the next day and sat with her while she gave the statement. The police woman guided her through the procedure, prompting her to mention each hoax call she could remember, starting with the one to her flat. Alice was asked if she had any ideas who might be responsible.

'Not really.'

'The first one was made by your ex-boyfriend, Tony Salmon wasn't it?'

'Yes.'

'Have you had any contact with him since?'

'No, well he's called me a few times.'

'How many?'

A lot of times and he'd called her parents and Kate. Lying to the police wasn't going to help anyone. 'I didn't keep a record, but he rang quite often to start with and tried my family too. He's stopped that now though, hasn't he?'

Alice's mum nodded her agreement.

'He's been harassing you in fact?'

Alice shrugged. She supposed he had.

'And he's visited you at work?'

'Yes.'

'And would he have known anything about the warehouse, that there was metal shelving for instance?'

'He came with me to a Christmas party.'

The police seemed convinced Tony was responsible for all the hoaxes and she had to admit they were probably right. It wasn't a nice thought at all, but at least now they'd be able to stop him.

It was such a relief to get away, that part felt almost as important as the fact she'd be alone with Hamish for days, and nights, on end. No one would know where she was and Hamish would look after her.

When he'd seen her after the latest hoax she'd still been shaky and told him she didn't know who she could trust. He'd shown her his work rota and compared it with the times of the hoaxes. Hamish had been at work when three of the calls were made and cutting someone out of a car for one of them. Although she'd never suspected him it was nice there was proof.

On the journey up to Wales they didn't discuss the calls or work. Instead he told her about his previous visits to the cottage they'd be staying in. It had been derelict when his cousin had bought it and Hamish and his brother Donald had helped renovate it. As payment they got to use it pretty much whenever they wanted.

'Do you do that often?'

'Yes. I've never spent a whole week there before though, not since we finished the work. Interesting as the birds are, I've usually had enough of just them for company after a few days.'

Ah, so she was the first girlfriend he'd brought here? And the first he'd taken to the sanctuary in Beaulieu. Even though Louise had made it clear he'd had plenty of girlfriends it did seem that he wasn't treating her as just the next one in a long line. That thought put a smile on her face.

'Wales is half a mile ahead, Alice. I want you to take a big breath, then blow out all your worries and leave them this side of the border. Right, go.'

Obediently she took a deep breath. 'I think that worked! It's just you me and the birdies now.'

'And maybe seals.'

'Really? I'd love to see a seal.'

'Then I'll do my best to find you one. In return you can find me a chuff.'

At least, that's what she thought he said. Presumably it was a bird, but it wasn't one she'd heard of or seen in a book. She'd not done a lot of research, but it was such a daft sounding name she thought she'd have remembered. Still, if he wanted to see one, she was happy to help him look. 'Deal.'

Hamish pulled up outside a fabulously rugged stone cottage.

'Here we are. Home sweet home.'

'Sweet is right. It's lovely.'

'Shall we dump our stuff and go for a walk round?'

'OK.' He'd driven for over four hours with just a quick break for coffee and a sandwich, so she could understand him wanting to do that. And of course bird watching was one of the reasons they were there. Not the only one, but it would get dark around seven each evening, which gave them plenty of time for indoor activities, and as this was Wales there was a good chance they'd get rained in at least some of the time.

She took the bag with the fresh herbs her dad had potted

up for her from the back seat and asked where the kitchen was.

'First left.'

The kitchen had a terracotta tiled floor, wooden beams and plain white walls. The furniture was all wood too, possibly antique, but the cooker and fridge were gleaming modern brushed aluminium.

Hamish brought in the cool box. 'Can I get you to deal with this?'

'No problem.'

She unloaded the contents into the fridge as he carted in everything else they'd brought with them. He clearly liked bacon and sausages! There was a good choice of other savoury ingredients though and a chocolate cheesecake, pots of strawberry mousse and a big tub of clotted cream.

Alice had brought food too, including the ingredients for cakes and cookies; she'd noticed he had quite a sweet tooth. She'd not started to unpack that box when he reappeared to see if she was ready to go.

'Yep, almost. The bathroom is where?'

'First door through there.'

'Thanks. Could you grab my coat and boots?'

'They're in the hallway.'

At the end of the hallway was a very short flight of stairs which presumably led to the bedrooms; the cottage seemed to have been built into the hillside. The massive bathroom was just before the steps and had a huge free-standing bath. Alice hoped she'd get the chance to use it. As she rejoined Hamish she caught sight of the living room. That too was painted white and furnished with wooden cupboards and tables. The sofa, in a deep cream which matched all the curtains she'd seen so far, looked very comfortable. So did the fluffy rug laid invitingly in front of a proper fireplace. The cottage was warm and she'd seen radiators, but hopefully they'd light the fire too. Alice very much liked the look of everything she'd seen.

She liked the sight of his coat hanging next to hers too. She wondered if her suitcase was also nestled against his in a bedroom. There was presumably more than one of those if Hamish, his brother and cousin all stayed there together.

During the walk Hamish pointed out the various habitats which meant they had a good chance of seeing a wide range of birds and other creatures. Alice learned 'chuffs' were very rare.

'How will I know it when I see it?'

'They're corvids.'

'You're not helping.'

'Crows with red beak and legs.'

'Sounds like an oyster catcher on steroids.'

Hamish laughed and pulled her close. 'I so love that description! Show me an oyster catcher on steroids and you'll be rewarded.'

'How?'

'I'm pretty good at massage.' The grin and raised eyebrows told her it wasn't just her shoulders he was promising to get his hands on.

'Give me those binoculars now. I've got red footed corvids to hunt down,' she said.

## Chapter 15

There was a cold wind blowing up over the cliff, which whipped Alice's hair back off her face and gave her a feeling that she too were held up by it, soaring as effortlessly as the seabirds. There was no danger of her joining them though, Hamish took care she stayed to proper paths and away from the crumbling cliff edges.

They didn't spot any steroid enhanced birds of any species, nor any seals that first afternoon, but the sight of gannets circling overhead then swooping down the cliff face and plunging into the sea delighted Alice. Like the oyster catchers they were smart looking birds; mostly white with neat black tips to their wings. Hamish pointed out the differences between them and the similar fulmars and herring gulls. Fulmars were grey across almost the whole of their topsides, the gulls had grey wings, pink legs and dark tails. Neither of those birds had the yellow head, clearly visible through binoculars, of the gannet. Even without that clue, Alice was soon able to distinguish the gannets by their distinctive, incredibly fast, dives for food.

'How many fish do they eat each?' she asked.

'I don't know. Depends on the size I suppose.'

'I was wondering if they got one every time... they do have a reputation for eating a lot.'

'I shouldn't think they get one every time.'

They watched, trying to determine if any gannets definitely caught a fish. It was difficult to tell as they travelled some distance under the water before emerging. A small fish could probably be swallowed without them noticing.

'There. That one did, I think,' Alice said when a bird appeared to swallow a couple of times as it surfaced.

They stayed out until darkness and hunger drove them back to the cottage.

'I'll get the fire going,' Hamish said as they removed their boots.

'I'll put the rest of the food away.' Alice did that, then started making plans for a meal. Between them they had everything needed for a fish stew. She assembled the ingredients on the sturdy kitchen table, noticing as she did that the fridge now held several bottles of wine, including one of champagne. She found a suitable pan, chopping board and knife and began work on an onion.

'Can I help?' Hamish asked.

'If you can peel potatoes.'

'I can.' He demonstrated by deftly preparing a large quantity of them.

Alice sautéed the onion as he skinned and chopped the fish.

'What do you want done with the... what is that thing, a chorizo?'

'It is.' She'd brought a couple with her; they were one of her current favourite ingredients. 'Do you like it with fish?'

'Never tried it, but I'm willing to give it a go.'

'Slice it thinly then, the rest won't need much cooking.'

He did as she asked and then slid the pieces into the pan. Alice cut a carrot into thin strips and added that, the potatoes, a can of butter beans and plenty of seasoning.

'Is there any wine or anything I can add to this?'

'I'll open a bottle, any preference?'

'Not the champagne.'

'You don't like it?'

'I do, but it seems a waste to put it in a stew.'

He removed a bottle from the fridge. 'We'll use this then, it was on special offer.' He opened it and poured some into a glass. 'Want to try it?'

'Yep.' She took a sip. 'Not bad at all.'

Hamish took the glass and tried it. 'No, it's OK. How much shall we put in?'

'We need enough liquid to cover everything, but we can make it up with water.'

He poured in enough to just cover the vegetables, which was almost half the bottle. 'What's next?'

'We give that fifteen minutes or so, just till the potatoes are soft, then add the fish and some fennel if you like that. Another five minutes and it'll be done.'

'Is this the fennel?' He picked up the pot of fennel seedlings and when she nodded, nibbled a feathery leaf. 'Hmmm, aniseed. Shall I chop it?'

'I usually just snip it in with scissors.'

'Nothing for me to do but pour us a drink then.' He found two flutes and opened the champagne. As they clinked glasses he said, 'To the start of things.' His eyes sparkled brighter than the wine.

When she put down her glass to stir the stew, Hamish

placed his next to it, moved behind her and put his arms around her. She leaned back against him and they stayed like that until she'd added the fish. Then he cleared away the things they'd used to prepare the meal and laid the table for them to eat.

The food was good and as neither of them had eaten properly all day it was soon gone. They didn't say much. Not because she was worried about saying the wrong thing, but because they didn't seem to need words to express their pleasure in being together. Alice guessed that like hers, Hamish's mind was mostly focussed on what was to come next.

When they'd finished the stew, Hamish offered dessert.

The cheesecake looked nice, but if she ate anything else now she'd feel uncomfortable if things started to get steamy. 'Maybe later.'

'Coffee?' His grin warmed parts of her the hot drink wouldn't reach and looking into the depths of his almost sea green eyes sent shivers through the rest of her body.

Unsure that she'd actually be able to speak she just nodded and pointed to her champagne, hoping he'd work out what she was saying yes to.

He picked up both glasses and took them into the living room. Alice joined him on the sofa in front of the fire. She took a large gulp of wine. Just as well because she almost knocked it over when she put it back down. He hadn't actually said anything about sharing a bedroom; he did want that, didn't he? Yes he must do. There was no doubting he was attracted to her and nothing he'd said indicated he hadn't expected her to jump to the obvious conclusion about his invitation to share a week in a remote cottage with him.

Hamish put his arm around her shoulder. 'Comfy?'

'Hmm.' She snuggled up to him and tried to relax.

Would she be a disappointment? He'd seen her in her most revealing dresses and had his arms around her... his hands on her... so he knew she wasn't skinny but he'd never seen her without dresses cut in a flattering style and curve enhancing underwear. She wasn't even wearing a particularly nice set as she'd dressed for comfort during the drive. And she'd had it on all day. What Alice needed was a shower. That'd leave her sweet smelling, dressed to be undressed and knowing if he'd put her suitcase in the same room as his own bag.

'After eating like a gannet, I don't exactly want to jump into the sea, but I could do with a shower,' she said.

'Sorry, no shower.' Hamish said. 'There is a bath. It's big enough for two.'

'Better go fill it then, hadn't you?'

'Yes, Ma'am.'

She followed him.

'I've put your stuff in here,' he went up three steps, pushed open the bedroom door and then headed back down to the bathroom.

Alice stepped into the room, which was also painted white and had wooden beams. There was a carved wardrobe and chest of drawers in the same warm brown wood as all the other furniture in the cottage. The room though was almost completely filled by the double bed. On that lay both their bags. So far so good. She extracted her wash bag, tiny silk nightie she'd bought the day before and her dressing gown, then quickly put her clothes away. Should she unpack for him? Hearing the water stop running made her mind up about that and she went down to the bathroom.

Candles gave the room a soft light and gentle vanilla fragrance. Hamish was waiting for her, still dressed and holding their wine glasses.

'Want me to scrub your back?' he asked.

'Yes please.'

'I'll just go and make sure the fire's safe to leave.' He put the glasses where they'd be in reach once the bath was occupied.

Alice quickly undressed and climbed into the enormous bath.

Hamish returned and picked up a loofah. 'It'd be easier if I got in there with you.'

'Like you said, there's plenty of room for two.'

When Hamish began undressing, Alice suddenly felt shy and ducked under the water. When she surfaced he was in. As well as back scrubbing, they washed each other's hair, rinsing it with the shower over the bath. She didn't point out he'd got her in there under false pretences.

It was relaxing to lie back against him in the warm water and enjoy the last few sips of champagne. Well relaxing-ish. He might be behaving patiently, but part of him was clearly eager to move on from the getting clean stage to something more exciting. That seemed a pretty good idea, but then so did taking things slowly and enjoying a gradual build up.

Hamish got out first. He wrapped a towel round his waist and fetched a bigger one he'd put to warm, for Alice. He draped it around her shoulders, then used a smaller one to squeeze some of the water from her hair. He let it fall to the floor and his arms drop to her side. He slid them inside her towel and pulled her close. Slowly, he bent his mouth to hers. Far too slowly. She stood on tip-toes to reach him. He kissed her incredibly gently until she was shaking with desire for him.

'It's warmer in the other room,' he said. 'Let's dry off in front of the fire.'

Alice secured her towel to give the effect of a very short mini dress and went into the living room where the crackling logs provided light as well as warmth. She smiled as she heard him blowing out the candles in the bathroom before following her.

'How are your feet after all that walking in your new boots?' he asked.

They were just a little tender in places, but she didn't intend to be on them much longer. 'They're OK. I've been wearing them in at home.'

She tried for another kiss, but he shook his head. 'I'd better take a look.'

Alice sank down onto the fluffy rug and extended a foot for his inspection. How long did he intend to keep her waiting?

'Hmm, bit red here. Have you got any moisturiser?'

'Yes.' She scrambled up and fetched it.

Hamish worked body lotion into her feet and as promised was pretty good at massage. As she'd hoped, he didn't stick to just one area of her body. He rotated her ankles and massaged the spots where the cuffs of her boots had made contact. Then he squirted lotion onto one shin, smoothed it over her lower leg and kneaded her tired calf muscles.

'That feels good,' she whispered.

He repeated the operation on the other leg, then his hands travelled up past her knees to her thighs. Just when she was positive the sensual movements were about to become definite foreplay he stopped and moved so he was behind her. She was sure she heard him chuckle at her groan of frustration.

'You seem a bit tense,' he said, his breath warm against her neck.

'Something like that.'

'I know what will help.' He began working on her shoulders

It was wonderful, but she needed more.

'Hamish, please!'

'Something you want?'

'You.'

'I'm all yours.' He eased her shoulders back until she was lying flat out on the soft rug. He knelt alongside her and unfolded her towel as through unwrapping a precious and fragile object, even though by then it wasn't covering much anyway.

'Alice, you're beautiful.' He stroked her cheek then slid his hand down her throat and onto a breast. He caressed it gently, then moved his hand lower.

She reached for him, pulling his mouth onto hers. His kisses started gently, but became ever more intense until she pulled her mouth away to insist, 'Now, Hamish. Now.'

He released her. Was he going to make her beg? No, just putting on a condom.

They made love in the flickering firelight. It wasn't like her fireman fantasy. It was better. So much better.

Afterwards they shared a wedge of chocolate cheesecake, eating it naked in front of the fire. Hamish's fine blond hair was already dry and the way the flames backlit it made his curls glow almost like a halo. If he let it grow any longer, he'd look almost like an oversized cherub. She tried to suppress the giggle that thought created.

'Would you like coffee now, or shall we go straight to bed?' he asked.

'What do you think?'

'That you'll want the bathroom first.'

'Of course.'

'Get on with you, then.'

As she left the room, she heard him pulling the fire guard away so he could attend to the dying embers. Hamish would keep her safe.

She was as quick as she could be in the bathroom and took her nightie with her to the bedroom. She slipped into it, gave her hair a blast with the hair dryer and combed it through. As she arranged herself on top of the bed in what was hopefully an enticing manner, Hamish came in; still naked.

He lay on the bed next to her and slipped a finger under the delicate shoulder strap of her nightie. 'Playing hard to get now, are we?'

'No. And I hope you're not going to either.'

'Well I'm hard.' He was too. 'And willing to play. Come get me if you like.' He rolled onto his back, put his hands behind his head and closed his eyes.

Alice just looked at him for a moment. He was gorgeous, he'd said he was all hers and it looked as though she had permission to do whatever she liked to him. She straddled his hips and took him inside her. For a few seconds his only reaction was to open his eyes wide and grin even more wickedly, but soon it became a game for two players.

Alice didn't think life could get much better and there were another whole five days of this to come.

## Chapter 16

The next morning Alice learned that, although having hot sex with a member of the emergency services did indeed cure any emotional issues a person might have, doing it whilst your hair was still damp left you looking like several pairs of fishnet stockings had exploded over your head. She discovered this fact after Hamish, already dressed, ruffled it up even more and declared, 'I'm not taking the blame for that!' She didn't need a mirror; the bits she could see to either side of her face were quite enough to make the point.

'You so are!'

'Really? Shall I leave you alone tonight so you have time to attack it with a steam iron or whatever you usually do?'

'No, I'm sure it'll be fine.' She attempted to pull it straight.

'It already is fine. Totally wild, but fine. Anyway, once we get outside the wind will mess it up again.'

'Good point.'

When she got to the bathroom she saw her hairstyle was even more bizarre than she'd imagined. Wasn't there a Greek goddess or something who had hair so scary it turned men to stone? Alice reckoned she could give her a run for her money. Actually, the way she was feeling she could compete with any goddess. Other than her hair she looked pretty good. Her cheeks were rosy from the wind the day before and her eyes sparkled from the evening's activities. She'd slept really well for the same reason and, she checked the watch she'd left in the bathroom, for about ten hours! No wonder Hamish had enough time to clean up the bathroom and she could smell breakfast cooking.

When she joined him he was reading a book. He seemed to have everything ready and to have been waiting for her. She'd only washed, slathered on moisturiser and the minimum of make-up and run a wet comb through her hair before dressing; she was going to have to learn to get ready much more quickly. Still, at least Hamish didn't seem the sort to tut disapprovingly if she'd not managed to get her hair dead straight or that her nail polish didn't go with her lipstick or worse, had a chip. Alice gave her fingernails a quick check. Perfect.

'You OK?' Hamish asked.

'Absolutely.' She gave a bright smile to prove it. 'What are you looking up?'

He handed her the book, which was open at the page for choughs and pushed a mug of tea towards her. Choughs, chuffs... did all Welsh birds have daft names? Thankfully she'd taken a swig of tea as she read, so it dawned on her the two were the same thing before she'd asked the question. There was a line drawing of the bird, which she didn't think would be much help in identification even if the thing were perched on the kitchen table waiting for toast.

'How many eggs?' Hamish asked.

'Eggs?' She'd seen enough sausages, bacon, tomatoes, fried bread and mushrooms to feed a family.

'From chickens, I promise. I haven't just gone and raided a gannet's nest.'

'I believe you, it's just I'm not used to a cooked breakfast.'

He turned away.

She moved over to him and tentatively squeezed his shoulder. 'Sorry, I didn't mean I didn't want it.'

He kissed her cheek. 'I knew you couldn't refuse my sausage.'

He wasn't annoyed then? But of course he wasn't Tony and not everyone sulked when they'd done something unexpected which wasn't greeted with total delight. Really she should stop expecting him to be like Tony... and she should stop behaving like Tony's girlfriend.

'I can't,' she agreed. 'One egg please and I'd like some of your mushrooms too.'

'If that's a euphemism it sounds a bit kinky, so obviously I'm up for it.' He winked. 'Maybe we'd better wait until after breakfast though, it's nearly ready.'

'Fair enough.'

He dished up the food, all of it looking perfectly cooked including the eggs.

'I'm impressed. The only times I've tried I broke them.'

'I get plenty of practice. We take it in turns cooking for our watch and as everyone loves a fry up, we have that a lot.'

Alice ate a lot more breakfast than she thought she'd manage, but nowhere near as much as Hamish got through.

'Your turn to wash up,' he told her when they'd finished.

He was right; there was no sign of last night's dinner dishes. She quite liked that she was expected to help out, not being treated just as a guest.

'Once you've done that, how long before you can be ready to leave?' he asked.

'Leave?'

'The choughs won't come to us.'

'Right. No, of course not. I'm ready, just need to put on thick socks and a jumper.'

'Excellent. Just leave everything on the rack to drain.'

Hamish made hot chocolate in the microwave and filled a flask, dropped the spoon and jug into the sink for her to wash, then left the kitchen. He'd returned by the time she had the plates and pans clean.

'All done,' she said. Then, 'Ah,' when she saw he was holding her crazy orange jumper, a pair of bright pink fluffy socks, boots and coat. 'Will it totally mess up your schedule if I use the toilet first?'

'Thirty seconds. Twenty-nine, twenty eight...'

She was pretty sure he was kidding, but ran anyway. No way would she be back before he'd finished, but if she didn't put on some hand cream and lip-salve she'd have rough skin and chapped lips all day. Surely hands soft enough to slide over his body and kissable lips were worth waiting for? She'd better do what she said she was going to do too; the beautiful scenery probably didn't come with en suite facilities.

'Minus one million and three, minus one million and four,' he said as she returned to claim her warm clothes.

'You're definitely exaggerating. A million and four seconds is two hundred and seventy-seven hours and two minutes and even I don't take that long.'

'You don't?' He gave a mock astonished expression.

'No. I expect it'll take you longer to work out I'm right and be impressed by my mathematical genius.'

'You're right and I'd need paper and pencil. Come on, jumper, socks, boots.'

'Gosh you're bossy.' She put on her socks.

'I am, but today I have an excuse.'

'Oh?' She pulled her sweater over her head, flicked her hair free and immediately wished she hadn't. It had probably looked better like that and wouldn't have blown about.

'The tide.'

'I thought you said choughs were most likely to be seen over grass.' Alice laced up her left boot.

'You'll see.'

Alice laced her right boot. 'Just my coat and I'm good to go.' She could put on her gloves, hat and scarf as she walked. She didn't have to though as once he'd locked the cottage door he unlocked the car.

'There's a good spot to see them a few miles further along the coast and as the weather isn't guaranteed to be this good later in the week, I think we should go today.'

'Fine with me.' She struggled into her coat; not easy with the seatbelt on. 'So describe them to me again.'

'Choughs?'

'Yes, them.'

'They're crows. If you see them in flight, which is most likely if we see them at all, the wings look like they have fingers, and the tail will be spread out like a fan. They're black all over except for the legs and beak which are about the colour of your lovely jumper.'

'You like it?'

'Yep. Well, I like that you have it more than the thing

itself. A girl who'd wear that on a date obviously isn't someone who takes themselves too seriously.'

'And you thought I might do that?'

'Seriously perhaps isn't the right word. I'd only ever seen you perfectly dressed, made up and with not a hair out of place. I mean you looked good, you always look good, but you also looked a bit high maintenance. I liked that you'd wear something fun but a bit odd if it kept you warm. Made you seem like the sort of girl who'd borrow completely loony wellies to wade through mud and who could survive in a Welsh cottage for a few days without needing to visit a salon or something.'

'Ah.' She was both of those girls. For the last couple of years Tony had kept one of them suppressed. She'd let that happen, but she'd learnt something from her mistake.

Hamish indicated and slowed to turn into a car park. If she was going to make her point, she'd better do it now. 'Yes, I can do that, but not all the time. I like to wear nice clothes, have smooth shiny hair and get made up, and all that takes time. I can be quick, but I won't always want to. OK?'

He just looked at her for what seemed a long time. She felt herself blushing, but held his gaze. She really wanted things to work out between them, but for that to happen she had to be the real Alice Bakewell, not a watered down version she hoped he'd approve of.

'Yes, OK.'

It felt like they'd made a pact.

Hamish carried a small rucksack and gave Alice his binoculars. They walked along a cliff path, stopping occasionally to scan the heather covered ground in search of choughs.

Alice spotted four crow type birds strutting about. She raised the binoculars. She couldn't make out any red bits, but they were definitely black all over. 'Is that them?' She handed over the binoculars.

He looked where she was pointing.

'Just to the left of that green bushy thing,' she said.

'Four together?'

'Yes.'

'Half a point. Right family, but they're carrion crows. Choughs are that shape and size and they're likely to be in groups too, but you'd see the red beaks and legs from here.'

'Carrion crows are what Sausage-Snowball is, aren't they?'

'Have another point, young lady. Even though I know you've been trying to lure him away from me.'

'Didn't need to try.' So he did know she'd been back to the sanctuary. Odd he'd not said, but then neither had she. Maybe he, like her, didn't want to make a big deal out of it. Suited her; she'd go sometimes if she felt like it but didn't intend to feel pressurised into making it too regular an occurrence.

When they reached the highest part of the cliff he gave her back the binoculars.

'Where should I look?'

'Behind you and down.'

Not sure if he was kidding, she turned and looked down. 'Oh!' There were seals; dozens of them. She used the binoculars. 'Awww, they're so cute. Look at their lovely whiskers and those sad puppy dog eyes.'

Hamish told her they were grey seals and when they all came onto the beach like that, it was known as a haul.

'I can see why. There's one coming out now and he really is hauling himself along. Don't get the grey bit though, speckled seals would suit them better.' She continued to watch them, laughing as one scratched itself and another rolled over a bit to raise one flipper off the ground. 'Look, that one's waving at us. Oh sorry...' She handed him the binoculars.

They took turns in watching the seals, pointing out any interesting activity to each other. In truth the seals didn't do very much, but were entertaining nevertheless.

'I've only ever seen the odd one in the sea with just his head showing, before,' Alice said. 'They always seem like they're watching whoever is watching them.'

'They probably are. My cousin is a wildlife cameraman and says that when he's walking amongst them it can be hard to get natural looking footage as they always turn to face him.'

'So, it's normal for them to be out the water like this?'

'Yes, they spend a lot of time out of the water. It's warmer for them, I think. At high tide they're obviously closer to the cliff and so harder to see from up here and they only use quiet beaches where people rarely go, so unless you're in the right place at the right time, you would only see them in the water.'

So he'd been in a hurry so she didn't miss seeing the seals, not because he was impatient to see the choughs... and she'd given him the 'you'd better get used to waiting for me' lecture. Ooops.

As they watched, the tide crept in and the seals hauled themselves higher up the beach until they were lost from view.

'That's your lot for today. If the weather keeps dry we can come back another day.'

'I'd like that. Thank you for bringing me to see them.'

'No problem. You do owe me a chough though.'

If one of them was payment for last night's massage, Alice was hoping to see a flock large enough to keep her in credit for the next seventy years. He'd said they were rare; were there that many in the country? She asked Hamish.

'There are about three hundred and fifty breeding pairs.'

'Nowhere near enough.' If they spotted every single one, that still worked out at less than once a month.

'No, it's a shame. Efforts are being made to increase the population and at least numbers do seem to be holding steady, which is good.'

'Yes.' She supposed people didn't light candles and run baths for the birds. Probably they just made sure they had plenty of food and had somewhere private to go. Which reminded her, she might have eaten a massive breakfast, but that was hours ago and they'd walked quite a way since then, all of it uphill. 'Have you got chocolate in that rucksack?'

'I might have.'

'Did you know that chocolate eating is a well-known aid to chough spotting?' Alice asked.

'No, but I'll bow to your superior knowledge in the matter.'

'Very wise; I know a lot of uses for chocolate.'

'Sounds promising.' His face was doing that trying and

failing to look innocent expression she liked so much.

'It's too cold to melt out here.' Oh rats, she'd just admitted she knew what was on his decidedly naughty mind.

They found a suitable rock to sit on and Hamish produced both the flask of drinking chocolate and a bar to eat. So far she calculated he was way ahead of her on points.

'So is this really a good spot to see your choughs, or shall we go somewhere else?'

'There's a reasonable chance of finding them here and as we're here already and there's plenty more to see, we might as well carry on. If your feet are up for it we can go down to the beach the other side of this hill then loop round inland back to the car.'

'OK, let's do that.' Her feet might not thank her, but if she didn't burn off the calories she was going to eat this week then they'd soon have more to complain about.

They continued along the coastal path, which got steeper the closer they got to sea level. The last bit was such a scramble she was glad they weren't going back the same way. Hamish went ahead, stopping frequently to check she was OK.

'I'm fine as long as I go slowly,' she told him.

'There's no rush at all.'

They stopped several times to look at different birds. In addition to those they'd seen already they spotted kittiwake, cormorants, Manx shearwater, razorbills and oyster catchers. Alice enjoyed looking at them, but didn't pay much attention to memorising distinguishing features. Staying upright and not twisting her ankle were taking priority in the concentration area of her brain. When they reached the beach, more oyster catchers raced about on the shore and 'chatted' to each other exactly as the ones at the sanctuary had done.

'Do you think they came to see me?' Alice asked.

'Nope. They have just one thing on their mind.' He indicated a pair of mating gulls. 'Disgraceful, isn't it? Who'd spend all their time eating fish and having sex?'

'No idea.' Alice grinned. 'By the way, how about tuna pasta for dinner tonight?'

'You're a bad, bad girl and I like you very much.'

She felt the same way about him. Maybe it was time to tell him so.

**Chapter 17**

The path away from the beach was, of course, up-hill again; a fact Alice had tried not to think about on the way down. It wasn't that steep, but it was long. She made good use of the binoculars as a chance to get her breath back during the climb. Twice she saw birds she thought could be choughs, but were proved to be more carrion crows when Hamish looked. Once he was sure he saw a pair of them, but by the time she'd focussed on the area they were gone and he couldn't find them again.

Alice had been a bit worried she'd get bored birdwatching, but she was enjoying herself far more than she'd imagined. She wouldn't want to move up here permanently, but it was a nice feeling that her phone was off for the next few days, that she didn't have to go anywhere or do anything other than follow Hamish and look at the view.

'Sorry, it's further than I remembered,' Hamish said during the long walk back across the heathland.

'That's OK, as long as the 'no rush at all' thing still applies?'

'It does,' he assured her. 'More chocolate?'

'Best idea you've had since your last good idea.'

'Which also involved chocolate, if I recall correctly.'

'Quite a lot of good ideas do,' Alice pointed out.

'But not all?'

'Oh no, definitely not all.' Some involved lovely fluffy quilts and a certain fireman out of uniform.

This time their seat was a tree stump. As Hamish poured their drinks and fished in the bag for the remains of the chocolate bar, Alice did a sweep with the binoculars. More crows swooped a little way off. The way they twisted and turned, sometimes seeming to perform loop the loops, made it appear they were showing off their acrobatic skills just for her benefit. With feathers splayed out like fingers on the tips of their wings it was easy to imagine they were waving a casual acknowledgement of her appreciation. They were smart looking birds. Not as elegant as the oyster catchers, but the classic black plumage made a statement and was set off to perfection by the red of their beaks. Red!

'Hamish,' she hardly dared to whisper in case the birds heard her and soared away from view. She slowly moved the binoculars away from her eyeline towards his and gestured, with a tiny movement, in the direction of the birds.

'Where? Oh, I've got them.'

'Are they...?'

'Yes. Yes, definitely choughs.'

Watching his face was even better than watching the birds chase each other through the air in synchronised twists and arcs. She did look at them too though, without the aid of binoculars, as she drank her chocolate. Hamish would probably want to talk about the sighting; she knew she would in his position. Plus she needed to check there were enough to keep her in massages for the rest of the trip. There were, and one left over for after they got home.

'Here.' Hamish gave her the binoculars.

When she looked again she tried hard to fix their exact shape in her mind, so she'd be quicker to recognise them if she saw any more. She handed the binoculars back as soon as he'd gulped down his drink, which must have been completely cold by then.

Hamish was able to study the birds for a few more minutes before they flew away.

'Seals and choughs in one day, we're doing well,' Alice said.

'You're good at finding things.'

It wasn't as though she could have missed the seals and she almost didn't realise it was choughs she was looking at, but she accepted the compliment. 'You'll have to take me on all your trips then, so you don't miss anything.'

'Starting to look that way. You know, I was a bit worried you'd get bored.'

'How could I when there's so much here to keep me entertained?' She snuggled close to him and kissed his cheek.

He gave her a proper kiss in return, then they continued the journey. By the time they got back to the car, the chocolate supplies were long gone, Alice's feet and legs were aching and the light was fading. She didn't creak as she got out again but felt as though she did.

'You OK?' he asked.

'Nothing a warm bath and soothing massage won't fix.' Some more hot sex wouldn't go amiss either. She might not be used to so much fresh air and spending hours on her feet, but she wasn't as tired as all that.

'If you don't mind macaroni cheese, you could soak in the bath while I get started on that. I'll come and scrub your back once it's in the oven.'

'Macaroni cheese has never sounded so appealing.'

He was as good as his word. Just as the novelty of lying in the big bath on her own was starting to ease off, he got in with her. She got her massage too, even if he spent less time on her shoulders, feet and aching calves than on the area between.

After they'd eaten and made love in front of the fire again, they cuddled up on the sofa for a while. As she'd guessed he talked about spotting the choughs, telling her that although he'd caught glimpses of them before, or seen them from a much greater distance, that day had been the first chance he'd had to really watch them.

'I'm glad I was there to share it with you,' Alice said.

'Me too. Is there anything else you'd like to do while you're here? There are enough walks and things to keep us busy, but if you fancy a change we could visit St David's or something. Are you interested in history?'

'A bit, I suppose.' Looking round a big house or castle might be fun, but she didn't want to spend all day in a museum unless it rained and there wasn't anything else to do.

'There are probably shops around somewhere.'

'Are you interested in shopping?'

'Not especially,' he admitted.

Alice was pleased. If they were honest with each other from the start, they'd be happier in the end, wouldn't they? 'We'll give that a miss then. If I get a shopping urge, I usually go with Kate.'

'Ah, good. I'm sure she's much more help than I'd be.'

'She chose the red dress I wore when we went to Tangs with your watch.' Oh, Red Watch. That colour was becoming a bit of a theme.

'Then she has excellent taste. Was the orange jumper her idea too?'

'What do you think?'

'I'm guessing not.'

'Even though that too is very tasteful, stylish and sophisticated?'

'Even though.'

'As it happens you're right.'

They didn't talk for a while, which was nice. Life didn't need to be all about making plans and bettering yourself, did it? Sometimes it was nice to just enjoy the moment.

'Hamish, there is something I'd like to do this trip.'

'Hmmm?'

'Would you carry me upstairs?' All three of them, but in her mind they'd be a tall ladder and the fire he'd be taking her away from wouldn't be safely retained in a grate.

'Are you really that tired?'

'It's not that.' She told him about her fantasy of being lifted over the shoulder of a handsome fireman and carried away from a fire, making it clear he more than qualified.

'I offered to do that at the New Forest Show. You needn't have put up with all the mud and birdwatching.'

'I was with Tony then. It's not right to carry out a fantasy, however innocently, with one man whilst dating another.'

'True.' He nodded as though acknowledging she had behaved properly. '...and the mud and birds?'

'I enjoy it, honestly. I wouldn't have thought I would except as a novelty, but I really do.'

'Good, because I thought it'd be nice to go out at dawn and listen to them singing, then walk out to St David's Head to look for choughs silhouetted against the sunrise.'

'In that case you'd better carry me up those stairs right now and give me something to help me sleep.'

He did.


The rest of the week was just as blissful. Well, perhaps getting up before dawn wasn't blissful in itself, but it was romantic watching the sunrise with Hamish and it was a lovely feeling to know she'd still be by his side at sunset. On the days at the end of the week when it rained they bought and wrote postcards. Alice also taught Hamish to bake scones and coconut cookies and he quizzed her on her bird identification.

Because the phone signal had been as bad as Hamish had warned her it would be, Alice had switched her mobile off and hadn't bothered charging it until their last night. She'd told everyone she'd be out of reach anyway, so didn't expect there to be many missed calls. There weren't, but most of the ones she did have were from Tony. There were also two texts asking her to call him.

Hamish dropped Alice off at her parents' home to collect her mum's car as arranged before she went to Wales. Alice's parents were pleased to see her, but had plans to go out so she didn't stay long. When she got home she found two notes from Tony pushed under her door. She ripped them up, wondering who he'd got to buzz him into the building while she was away. It wasn't unease over that which meant she felt lonely for probably the first time in her life. She missed Hamish already. Fortunately her loneliness didn't last long as Kate was keen to come round and hear all the details of the trip to Wales.

Alice described the way he'd surprised her with the seals and how cute they were.

'That's sweet. Go on.'

Alice explained about the scenery and the miles they'd walked and how she was sure her thighs were slimmer.

'Bonus. Go on.'

Alice told her about the gannets, choughs and oyster catchers.

Kate interrupted before she'd mentioned a quarter of the species they'd seen. 'Fascinating. Go on.'

Alice tried to tell her about the lovely cottage.

'Alice! You know these aren't the details I want.'

She did know of course, and wasn't deliberately keeping anything from Kate. They'd always told each other pretty much everything, but come to think about it, although there was no doubting that Pete made Kate very happy, she only spoke about him in vague terms. 'Well they're all the ones you're going to get. You've got Pete, you can fill in the blanks.'

'Like that, is it?'

'Like what?'

'You're in lurve.'

Alice couldn't deny it.

'Alice? Is this it? The real thing?'

'Yes. Yes, I think it is.'

Back at work, as they made coffee, her colleagues asked Alice if she'd had a nice break. She'd barely begun giving them the details she'd shared with Kate when the phone rang. No one moved to answer it. It wasn't so surprising they'd rather catch up on her gossip than get to work dead on nine in the morning, but there seemed more to their reluctance than that.

'What's up with you lot?' Alice demanded.

They looked decidedly uncomfortable. Emma and Lucy looked at Kath as though willing her to answer.

'Oh no, the hoaxes haven't stopped?' Alice said.

'No they haven't.' Kath picked up the phone. 'Tatisuz, good morning. How can I help...? Hold on.' Those last two words were said with none of the cheery professionalism with which she'd answered the call. Kath pressed the mute button. 'It's Tony. I'm guessing you don't want to talk to him?'

Alice shook her head.

'She doesn't want to talk to you, so please stop calling here and stop calling the fire brigade!' She banged the phone down.

Kath explained that there had been two more hoax calls since the paramedic had come expecting to find Alice trapped under fallen shelving in the warehouse. 'Tony kept calling too. We told him you were away for the week just to stop him.'

'Did it?'

'Yes and there haven't been any hoaxes since.'

Miles came out into the main office. 'Nice to see you back, Alice. Pop in for a chat will you, when you're ready.'

'I'll come now.'

Miles was very sweet, asking if she felt better after her ordeal and if she'd enjoyed her holiday. She answered yes to both.

'I'm sorry to have to tell you there have been a couple more hoax calls.'

'Yes, Kath said.'

'I want to assure you that I don't blame you in any way, but it does seem that this might all be more to do with you than with the company.'

She nodded.

'If there's anything you can think of which might help the police stop... whoever is responsible, then please let them know, or tell me if that's easier. And if you need time off to make a statement or anything...'

'Thanks, Miles. You don't have to be tactful, I know my ex-boyfriend seems to be the person responsible and I've already given the police one statement. If I think of anything else though, I'll pass it on. I want this person caught as much as anyone else.'

'I'm sure it will all be over soon and now there's some good news. I haven't told anyone else yet, but at last I can announce your pay rises.' He went back out with her and told the women they'd each be getting a fifteen per cent pay increase. 'The men are getting a raise too, but not quite the same amount, so I'd appreciate it if you were to be a bit discreet.'

'No problem,' Kath said.

Miles nodded and returned to his office.

Naturally that good news required a fair bit of talking about.

'Maybe we'll be able to get our kitchen sorted now,' Kath said. 'The units were getting ropey when we bought the place and that was so long ago I was skinny then!'

'I'll be able to pay off my credit card bill,' Emma said. 'And get some decent shoes.'

Lucy said she hoped to save most of her increase. 'What about you, Alice?'

'I think I'll get some binoculars.'

'Oh yeah? For the birds or the fire station?' Emma asked.

'From the smile on her face this morning, no binoculars are needed when it comes to firemen,' Kath said. 'She's not having any trouble getting up close and very personal, if you catch my drift.'

'I couldn't possibly comment,' Alice said.

Alice's phone beeped to tell her she had a text. It was from Tony asking to speak to her. She deleted it. For the rest of the day Alice found it hard to concentrate on work. None of the figures added up. Well they did; her maths didn't let her down but accurate as the results were they just didn't make sense.

Tony called her mobile at lunchtime and sent two more texts. She half expected to see him waiting when she got home, but there was no sign of him. He did try to call her again before she went out though. When Hamish picked her up she told him the hoaxes hadn't stopped and that Tony kept trying to speak to her.

'I knew about the hoaxes. Devon said so far there's nothing to prove who made any of them except that first one from Tony. The rest have all been made from public phones.'

'The same one?'

'No, different ones but all in this general area. The police are involved now too and they've even looked at CCTV footage from the times calls were made, but it's not been much help. They're not even positive they were all made by the same person, apparently in one the caller seems quite short.'

'Tony keeps ringing me. Trying to anyway, I haven't answered.'

'I thought he'd stopped that nonsense.'

'So did I. Actually this seems different. He was sending flowers and asking me to take him back. Now he just says he needs to talk to me.'

'What are you thinking?'

'I'm just not sure he's behind this. I know it looks like he must be, but it just doesn't seem like him. Not to keep on with it.'

'Were you surprised he made the first call?'

'I wouldn't have expected it, but he was upset and he'd been drinking, then to see us together... I'm not excusing him, obviously that's no excuse but I can sort of understand. He likes to get his own way, but he's logical. He'd have worked out by now I wasn't going to change my mind and this wasn't helping, wouldn't he?'

'You'd think so.'

'And that thing at work... that was really scary. You wouldn't frighten someone you cared about like that, would you?'

'I wouldn't and I don't think any sane person would.'

'And that call from the short person? He's not as tall as you, but I don't think he qualifies as short.'

'No.'

'If that was connected it couldn't be him and I just can't see him asking anyone to make a hoax call for him.'

'That bit is odd. You'd have to be really close to ask someone to do that, and for them to agree.'

'His friends are really colleagues and people he knows from the gym. Not the sort of person who'd commit a crime for him.' Rachel was the most likely, but it was impossible to imagine her getting involved and anyway, she wasn't short.

'A decent friend would try to stop him getting himself into trouble, not make it worse,' Hamish said.

Yes, that's what Rachel would do. 'Forget about her, Tony, ask me out instead,' was likely to be her line.

'Try not to worry, Alice. Proper investigations are going on, probably they're a lot further forward than what I've heard about.'

True, he'd only been back on duty for one shift. 'Perhaps you can take my mind off it?'

'I'll see what I can do.'

He didn't stay the night as he was on earlies the following

day and didn't want to disturb her when he got up, but he managed to ensure she had an untroubled night's sleep.

The next day she thought about their discussion of Tony. If he'd not made the hoax calls and he wasn't still trying to get her back, then why was he so anxious to talk to her? Perhaps he thought he'd left something important at her place, or maybe he needed to get his name taken off the phone contract or something else he'd set up for her? There were several perfectly good reasons for him wanting to get in touch and one simple way to find out. The next time he texted to ask to speak to her she replied to say he could come round that evening.

If Tony was surprised to see Kate when he came, it was nothing to Alice's reaction at seeing Rachel with him.

'We'd better all sit down,' Alice said. She didn't offer tea.

'It's about all these hoaxes, Alice,' Tony said. 'The police are involved now and they think I'm responsible.'

'I'm not surprised,' Kate said.

Tony ignored her and spoke directly to Alice. 'I know the one I made looks bad, but I swear it's the only one. It was a dangerous, reckless thing to do as well as the worst possible way to try to get you back. Having a fireman in here in the middle of the night was exactly what I didn't want.' There was no humour in his voice or face.

'Alice,' Rachel said, 'This could cause serious trouble for Tony at work.'

'It's hardly my fault! You don't think I enjoy being scared by some crazed stalker, do you?'

Kate put an arm round Alice's shoulder.

When she was calmer Alice asked why he'd been going to her place of work.

'It was another mistake to go there, I realise that.'

'Why keep doing it then?'

Tony denied being there other than when he'd spoken to her in the car park.

'I don't know what you want from me, Tony. I couldn't stop the investigation even if I wanted to and I don't, because I want whoever is responsible caught and stopped.'

'Me too, and not just because it will clear my name. I see this is horrible for you. I just wanted you to know it's not me. Maybe it will help you think of who else it could be.'

'I believe him,' Kate said after he'd gone.

'I don't know. There was no point to all that, unless I was supposed to suddenly get jealous of Rachel. If I had any information I'd have reported it already and he was lying about coming to work. Miles saw him at least twice.'

'You don't know that. He said he saw an Audi, but Tony isn't the only person who owns one. Besides I don't trust your boss.'

'What? He's been brilliant over this.'

'Hmm, well if he has it's the only thing. What about the pay rises he promised?'

'I forgot to tell you, we're all getting fifteen per cent.'

'That just makes me more suspicious.'

'What's got into you? You used to like him and hate Tony, now it's the other way round.'

'I never hated Tony. He was always good to you in his way and he's obviously really upset now.'

'Yes you did! You were always trying to wind him up and make him jealous.'

'OK maybe I was a bit hard on him, but I don't want him getting in trouble for something he didn't do. Rachel's right, this could be serious.'

'That's right, poor little Tony. Everyone feels sorry for him and it's all my fault.'

'I never said it was your fault.'

Kate tried to put her arm around Alice, but she shrugged her off. 'You were thinking it.'

'I'm going,' Kate said. 'Call me when you're in a better mood.'

Alice sat with her head in her hands when Kate had gone. Her sister had a point, she had got herself into a bad mood and snapped and she knew why. Although she'd thought all along that this wasn't something Tony would do, she'd been half hoping it was because if it wasn't him it was someone else. She didn't know what they wanted or what they might do next. Until they were caught, she was going to be permanently frightened.

Alice went to bed, but wasn't asleep when Tony rang at three in the morning.

'Should there be anyone at your work?'

'No and you shouldn't be either.'

'I was hoping to see whoever it was your boss saw hanging about and get the registration to prove it wasn't me. As I drove down the track I'm sure there were lights on and a car passed me.'

'If you think there's something wrong call the police.'

'But if there's not it'll look like another hoax. Alice, I know it's not your problem, but I've made a few mistakes at work through not concentrating and what with the warnings about the hoaxes I could lose my job. Please help me.' He sounded desperate.

She had the key to work and wouldn't sleep anyway. 'OK.'

'Perhaps you'd better bring your boyfriend.'

She couldn't as Hamish was on shift. She really should let someone know where she was going though. Her parents would worry and she didn't want to call Kate after their row and be accused of waking her up just because she distrusted Tony. She compromised by sending Kate a text and slipping a note under her neighbour Doris's door.

When Alice drove her mum's car into the car park just minutes later, she saw another car next to Tony's and the building open with all the lights on. One of her colleagues must have come by as Miles had asked. Wondering why they'd gone inside, Alice headed for the entrance.

As she stepped through the doorway Tony said, 'I'm so sorry, Alice.'

Then something struck the back of her head, she felt her body sink to the floor and everything went dark.

## Chapter 18

When she came round, Alice was soaking wet and in pain. She could hear a scratching noise and feel hot breath on her face. She fought to control her shivering and terror. They'd be OK, Devon would come soon to rescue them. She drifted away again.

When she came to for the second time she was still wet, frightened and hurt, but she remembered she was at Tatisuz, not back in the past, trapped with Frodo on a building site. She wasn't cold this time, but she was trapped and she didn't have the comfort of her dog with her. Alice attempted to wriggle herself free.

'Don't struggle. I'm trying to help you.' It was Tony.

Alice tried to scream, but no sound came. She felt sick and her throat was as raw as if she already had been. Her eyes stung. Her head hurt so much. What had Tony done to her?

'Alice? Alice can you hear me? There's a fire. We need to move.'

A fire? Like she'd believe that. How many hoaxes had he made now? It was so hot and her head hurt. Alice could see flames, just like at the cottage with Hamish. She tried to drift back to sleep, but Tony threw water over her.

'Alice, come on. I can't carry you. You've got to help me get you somewhere safe.'

It wasn't Tony who hit her, she remembered. He was inside the building. Whoever hit her must have been waiting behind the door. The building was on fire!

'We need to get out,' she croaked.

'The doors are locked. We have to go up, it's our best chance.'

She looked at him properly, her head swimming as she moved it. Even in the red smokey light she could see he was hurt; one arm dangled uselessly at his side and his head was bleeding. He staggered away from her. When he returned he had a washing up bowl which he emptied over her.

'Stop doing that.'

'There's petrol everywhere, Alice.'

As soon as he said it she recognised the smell. It was that, as well as the smoke, which was stinging her eyes.

'I've used all the extinguishers I could find and chucked water everywhere, but I couldn't put the fire out. If we get above the flames we might survive long enough for the fire brigade to rescue us.'

'When did you call them?' They must be nearly there. She didn't have to move.

'They took my mobile. Yours too, I checked. I couldn't find a phone.'

'They're upstairs, all except one over there,' she pointed to the red glow.

'Come on, then.'

'You go. I'm tired.'

'Alice, move, now!'

With his help, she crawled up the stairs to the offices and they pulled the door shut behind them before collapsing. The air was fresher inside and Alice gradually felt a little better.

'There's a fire escape up here.' She got herself over to the door and pushed the bar. It didn't budge. Alice grabbed it to help pull herself up, then threw her weight against it. Still nothing. She tried again without success. Tony had said the doors were locked. Whoever had knocked her out and started the fire must have blocked up the emergency escape too.

Now what? The phone line was dead, as was the electricity supply. It wasn't totally dark though. Light from the fire at the other end of the building showed at the windows. Alice located the extinguishers and pulled them over to where Tony was sprawled just inside the doorway.

'Tony? Tony are you awake?'

He opened his eyes. 'Alice? Are you OK?'

'I will be, we both will.' Good, he was conscious, but only just. Alice dragged him further into the room, then set all the extinguishers off, coating the walls and door with foam and soaking the floor with water in the hope of keeping the fire away.

Inch by inch she pulled Tony to the wall furthest away from the fire. She was gasping for breath. Just exhaustion or was the fire using up the available oxygen? Tony's breathing came in rapid little pants. Should she try to open a window? They had bars to keep thieves out, so doing that wouldn't allow them to jump clear and she knew fires needed oxygen. But so did they. After a struggle she forced open the nearest window and gulped in the fresh air.

'Is that better?' she asked Tony.

She couldn't make out his reply. His head was cut and arm damaged, maybe she should take a look? She tugged his jacket back and ripped his shirt to expose a gaping wound which was bleeding heavily. The cut on his head didn't seem too bad. Thankfully the first aid kit was nearby. She tipped everything onto the floor and tore open the packs of bandages. She covered his head injury, taping the dressing into place. She wadded up the triangular bandages into a pad and bound that over the deep gash in his shoulder. It wouldn't help much, there wasn't enough padding and she'd not managed to work the bandages round him well enough to keep them tight.

Pressure. You had to apply pressure to the wound and elevate it. Somehow she pulled Tony into what was almost a sitting position. This had to be hurting him, but he'd not so much as grunted. She could hear him breathing though, so placed the flat of her hand against the covering to his wound and allowed herself to slump forward so some of her weight was on it. Already she could feel blood soaking through.

There was nothing more she could do but wait and hope. She seemed to do that for a very long time. Someone would see the fire surely? They were a long way from the road, but at night the flames must be visible and the alarms might have triggered.

'Sirens,' Alice whispered. 'Tony, can you hear them?'

He didn't reply.

The sirens grew louder until she was certain they really were coming for them. The red light through the window was interspersed with flashes of blue. Alice hauled herself up to the window. She couldn't shout and waving wouldn't help, not yet as they were at the back of the building. She collapsed with one arm dangling out.

When she came to again Alice knew she was in hospital and remembered most of what had happened before the fire engine arrived. Her mum was there, holding her hand.

'Hi, Mum.'

'Alice.' She kissed her cheek with tears of relief running down her face. 'She's back with us, Peter.'

Her dad kissed her too and Kate squeezed her other hand.

'You're all right, love. Going to be at any rate,' he said.

'And Tony?'

'They're operating, love.'

A nurse shone lights in Alice's eyes, checked her blood pressure, asked her questions and told her to rest.

As soon as she was gone, Alice asked, 'What happened? Do you know?'

'Not much of it,' Kate said. 'I rang to complain your text woke me and didn't get any reply, so I tried Tony's number. Can't even remember why I had it, but I knew he used it for work so didn't think he'd have changed it. When he didn't answer either I suddenly felt like something bad had happened.'

'That's probably just when I got hit on the head.'

'Oh! Oh, that's spooky. Anyway, I came out to look for you, saw the fire and called 999.'

'Did Hamish rescue me?'

'No. He'd been called out to your flats. Another hoax.'

'Another one? That makes no sense.'

'No, it doesn't.'

'Hamish came to see you,' Alice's mum said. 'I told him to

go home and sleep and we'd let him know when you came round.'

Kate went out to call him, then suggested her parents also go home and come back later with clothes and other things Alice would need. 'I'll stay with her.'

Alice watched her sister fall asleep in a chair, then slept herself.

When she woke, Kate told her Hamish had been there for a couple of hours. 'I had to practically force him to go home and sleep. I thought you'd rather see him when you weren't both fighting to keep your eyes open.'

Although she wished he was still by her side, she could see Kate had acted for the best.

'Mum brought you loads of stuff. Hopefully you'll be out before you need half of it.'

'Is there any more news of Tony and what happened?'

'They've had to pin his shoulder and give him transfusions, but he's OK,' Kate said.

'Did you see him?'

'No. The police are questioning him. Asking him questions, I mean. They're not treating him as a suspect.'

'No, he saved me, Kate. He was badly hurt, but it was him who brought me round and got me up the stairs away from the fire. I think I'd have just given up, but he wouldn't let me and wouldn't leave me.'

A nurse came to test her responses again. 'You're doing fine,' she assured Alice.

'I am, but you must be exhausted, Kate. Go home and sleep.'

'I don't like to leave you.'

'I'm safe here and Hamish will be in later.'

Kate shrugged. 'All right. It's not as though you damaged anything important, just your head.'

That did more to reassure Alice she wasn't seriously hurt, than the nurse's words had. 'Go away, Kate.'

Hamish had been watching over her as she slept. He'd come back soon. Alice smiled and slipped into a dream of him carrying her somewhere safe. She woke to find Hamish leaning over her.

He kissed her cheek. 'Hello, sleeping beauty.'

'Hello.'

He sat on her bed. 'Jeff's going to be disappointed. He said if you were in one of those hospital gowns which don't do up he'd come and visit you.'

She shuddered.

'No brain damage then. If you'd taken that calmly I'd have been worried.'

'I'm going to be fine, apparently.'

'Good.' He kissed her. 'Don't give me another scare like that.'

'Now you know how I feel when you're on duty and I hear a siren or news report of a fire.'

'You're going to have to get used to that, my love.'

'Am I indeed?' She couldn't make herself sound indignant.

'Do you want to tell me about it, or would you rather not?'

'I'll tell you. It might help me make sense of it.'

When she had he said, 'You did brilliantly and it seems

Tony's not so bad after all.'

'No. Just not right for me. I suppose he'll be cleared of any connection with the hoaxes now?'

'Did you know there was another one last night?'

'Yes, to the flats.'

'It was made from Tony's phone.'

'No! But...'

'The call was recorded. They'll be able to tell it wasn't him.'

'They'll find whoever is doing this, won't they?'

'Yes. Yes they will.' He tried to talk of more cheerful subjects, but the conversation drifted back to the fire and he told her how worried he'd been when Doris, evacuated again from the flats, had read the note Alice left. She'd wondered aloud why Alice had gone to work in the middle of the night. Just moments later he'd learned there was a fire there.

'If I didn't already know how I felt about you, that would have told me.'

'And how do you feel?'

'I... oh to hell with the taking it easy and not rushing you, I love you. I want to marry you and spend the rest of my life with you.'

'I love you too.' Alice reached up to pull him close for a proper kiss.

Another wretched nurse chose that moment to come in and do her stuff with the torch and blood pressure cuff. Alice almost forgave her though when she said, 'You'll most likely be able to go home in the morning.'

When she'd gone, Hamish said, 'You'd be welcome to

come and stay at mine, but I know your parents want to look after you for a bit and I think that might be best.'

'I think so too.'

He told her about the way Kate had insisted on staying by her side.

'Proper big sister, bossy but looking out for you. She reminds me of my brother.'

'Ah yes. I'm looking forward to meeting Dastardly Donald.'

'I don't remember telling you he's dastardly.'

'He's your big brother, stands to reason.'


When her parents came to collect her, Alice asked to see Tony first. They found him propped up in bed with Rachel by his side.

'I've come to thank you. You saved my life,' Alice said.

'And you saved mine. Those thugs stopped beating me up when you arrived. When I saw them knock you out, I pretended I was unconscious too. I wasn't far off to be honest, but I was in a better state than if they'd hit me again. And then when I really did pass out you bandaged me up.'

'I'm not sure that did anything much.'

'It did. I was told that if I'd lost any more blood I wouldn't have made it and your first aid efforts made the difference.'

'Did you recognise them, the people who hit you?'

'No. I think I would now though. And I know... Oh! I'd forgotten. I saw their car. It was a Fiesta not an Audi, but I wrote down the registration. It's in my glove box. Rachel, will you get it and give it to the police?'

'No problem. Glad you're all right, Alice.'

When she'd gone, Alice kissed Tony's cheek. 'Thanks again. Are you going to be all right yourself?'

'They're letting me out tomorrow I think. Rachel's going to stay and help me.'

'Are you and her...?'

He didn't meet her gaze. 'Er, maybe. I think so.'

'I'm glad, Tony.'


Over the next few days, Hamish visited Alice regularly at her parents' home. He was kind, sweet and funny but didn't tell her again that he loved her. She'd been awake when he said those words, hadn't she? Alice had almost been killed, saved by her ex-boyfriend and the hoaxer was still making calls. Except he wasn't a hoaxer as the fire had been real... or was that started by someone else? It was hard to know what had been real and what hadn't.

Both Kate's and then Alice's birthday celebrations were unusually low key. As they were born two years and two days apart, the sisters had frequently competed to hold the best parties. This time though, Kate opted for a restaurant meal with just Alice, her parents, Pete and his mum and dad and Hamish. Alice found even that tiring, so asked for tea and cake at home with the same group of people.

She did justice to her mum's fabulous baking, especially the chocolate, beetroot and cinnamon birthday cake. Alice was confident she'd soon be able to put her birthday gifts to good use. Her parents gave her a three in one walking coat, which could transform from something close to a continental quilt into a light rainproof jacket by undoing a few zips and discarding sections. Hamish gave her a set of binoculars and a bird identification book. He'd put a marker in the page for choughs.

The present she was particularly looking forward to trying out was Kate's offering. She'd used her garish wellington boots as wrapping for a set of very nice underwear. The expression on Hamish's face suggested he approved. Her dad pretended to, or maybe really did, think it was a lacy blouse.

Her mum fussed over Alice constantly. When she started to find it overpowering, she knew she was recovering.

'Save me from her, Hamish,' she begged.

'As I didn't get to rescue you from the fire, that's the least I can do. Where do you want to go?'

'Somewhere peaceful.'

'The sanctuary? You could hide in a hide.'

'Sounds perfect.'

Since her ordeal Alice had been either lying or sitting down and the walk to the hide was far more tiring than she'd expected. Even sitting up properly on the bench so she could watch the oyster catchers seemed like hard work.

'Hello,' Louise's loud whisper reached them through the door.

'We're in here,' Hamish told her.

'I thought Alice might need coffee. It's not that warm today.' She produced a flask and packet of biscuits.

'Oh, thank you, Louise. That's kind,' Alice said.

'Glad to see you're out and about,' Louise said, then left. A moment later she put her head back in. 'The coffee shouldn't be too bitter. The state you're in I didn't think I'd need much poison.' Then she really was gone.

Alice burst into tears.

Hamish held her. 'Hey, come on. You're OK and you do know she was kidding?'

'I know and she was being nice.' Alice blew her nose. 'Sorry. I think it's having to be cheerful in front of Mum. I just needed to feel sorry for myself for a minute.'

'I feel sorry for you too.'

'Oh?' Is that why he'd said he loved her? Alice wanted to cry again.

'Yes, life with Jeff is a horrible thought.'

'Jeff?'

'Yes. I know you and Tony did most of the actual saving part, but it was Jeff who put you over his shoulder and carried you down the ladder out of the fire.'

'I don't even remember.' It was almost funny; her fantasy had come true but not only couldn't she remember it happening, she didn't want to; and Jeff being involved was the least worst part.

'Don't worry, he'll remind you. Constantly.'

'You mean I'm going to have to be grateful to Jeff?'

'Afraid so. Though maybe if you were unconscious at the time it won't count and you won't have to marry him?'

'I am not marrying Jeff!'

'Tony then? It really was him...'

'Don't be silly. I don't love Tony, I don't think I ever did and I definitely don't love Jeff. How could you think such an idiotic thing?'

'But he's a fireman and he saved you...'

'What's that got to do with anything? Oh, Hamish, my fantasy is just that. It never did stand up to reality. OK yes, you being a fireman didn't exactly discourage me, but if that was the only thing I liked about you I wouldn't have kept seeing you. Can you honestly see me lasting as much as one date with Jeff?'

'No. No I really can't. I was a bit worried though to start with. That kind of thing has happened to me before and you could have been on the rebound.'

She kissed him. 'I admit I wasn't entirely sure either to start with. Sounds like we were both holding back a bit.'

'Except in Wales?'

'True. Hamish, I love you.'

'I love you too.' He kissed her until she had to push him away for fear her dizziness would return.

'I wish I'd accepted your offer at the show now. I'd rather cling on to my rescue fantasy than remember I once needed it for real.'

'If it would help, we could have our honeymoon in the cottage in Wales and I could carry you up the stairs again.'

'Yes, that would help a lot.'

## Chapter 19

With the help of the registration number Tony had noted down, the police tracked the owner of the car which had been outside Tatisuz on the night of the fire. An officer came to see Alice at her parents' home.

'The person in question is a Mr Blair, does that name mean anything to you?'

'No. I don't think I know anyone of that name. It isn't anyone who works for the company, I'm sure of that. Did he see... or say, anything helpful?'

'He did, yes. When we called to say we were making routine enquiries about the car he made such a fuss we decided we should take a look at it. He'd left the petrol cans in his garage along with a computer and printer he'd taken from your office and a few boxes of stock. He soon confessed that he and his brother set the fire. When we said we had CCTV footage of them making the hoax calls they confessed to that too. They deny any violence though.'

'You don't believe them, do you?' Alice's dad asked.

'No, and as the fire exit had been deliberately blocked they'll never convince a jury it was accidental or unplanned. We'll get the truth out of them and the bloke who hired them.'

'Have you traced him?' Alice asked.

'Oh yes. It was your boss, Miles Molde.'

'Miles! But why would he want to burn down his own business?'

'It's not unheard of for people to do that, either an insurance scam or an attempt to cover something up.'

'I should have known!' Kate said.

'How could you?' Alice asked.

'I knew he'd been turned down for a big loan. I was worried about your job and looked at his accounts.'

'You never told me.'

'I couldn't. It's confidential and I had no idea at the time what it might mean. I did tell you I didn't trust him though. When you said he'd got a big order and later confirmed you were getting your pay rises I hoped everything was OK, but something bothered me.'

'It should have bothered me too. That pay rise was too good to be true. Orders were up a little, but transport and insurance costs had soared. None of the figures seemed to make any sense, but he always had some kind of explanation and I didn't properly look into it.'

'You mean this was all just an insurance scam?' her dad asked.

'Tax too I imagine as the company he was paying huge transport costs to is called Molde Motors,' Alice said. 'He made a big thing out of the coincidence.'

The police officer made notes and assured them he'd pass that on. 'You're right about the insurance part. Molde admitted that, but claims he had no idea anyone would get hurt.'

'Claims?' Alice's dad asked.

'We're assuming the original plan was to set a fire without trying to kill anyone, but when you two turned up they panicked. One of the brothers made that last hoax call from your friend Tony's phone. Presumably Molde told them what to say, so he had to know Tony was there. If he thought there would be a surviving witness he'd have called them off, so we reckon he knew someone was in the building when it went up.'

'And the other hoaxes? Did Miles arrange those?'

'Yes. He set off the alarms in the building himself and had the Blair brothers make the calls. He thought it might make the fire brigade less likely to respond to a genuine one, or at least slow them down so there wouldn't be any evidence and he hoped whoever made the first one would be blamed for everything. Once he discovered who that was, he tried harder to implicate him.'

Eventually the brothers were tried and found guilty of arson and attempted murder. Miles was convicted of fraud and his part in the attempt to kill Tony. It wasn't proven he'd known Alice's life was also in danger, but even so he received a long prison sentence.

Six months later, Alice was again back at her parents' house. She even slept in her old room as her dad had got rid of his wine making kit and taken up painting. Watercolours thankfully, so she only had to negotiate his easel, not inhale paint and thinner fumes.

There was a tap on her door.

'Come in.'

Her mum brought her a tray holding a cup of tea, croissant with jam, dish of strawberries, glass of juice and a pot of yoghurt. 'You might not feel like it, but try to eat something. It's going to be a busy day.'

'Thanks, Mum.'

'I'll leave you to get up and have your shower, but don't take too long. We need to leave for the hairdresser in an hour.'

'No problem. Mum, are you crying?'

'Yes, but the mother of the bride is supposed to do that. It's only because I'm so happy.'

'So am I, Mum. Really, really happy.'

'Well, I should think so.'

Kate was waiting downstairs by the time Alice was ready. 'Mum wouldn't let me come up, she said I'd distract you.'

Their mum drove them to the hairdresser's and then on to the beautician's to have their make-up and nails done. By the time they left for home all three of them were total glamour from the neck up. Alice's mum's hair was in a super sleek glossy bob. Her make-up subtle, but for the flash of deep red lipstick, perfectly matched by her nails. Alice and Kate's hair were controlled torrents of spring curls. Kate's was finished with a circlet of tiny cream rosebuds. Alice had in place a clip onto which her veil would later be attached. Their faces seemed to wear no make-up, though their complexions were flawless, their lips glossy and lashes even longer and thicker than usual. They'd both had classic French manicures.

'Do you think you can eat something, love?' Alice's mum asked as she turned onto the driveway. 'There's enough time.'

'Probably and I could do with another cup of tea.'

'I can definitely eat,' Kate said.

'I've made a quiche, but I could do you some sandwiches or soup or...'

'Quiche would be great, Mum,' Alice said.

'And maybe some cake?' Kate added.

As the kettle boiled there was a knock on the door. Her dad went to open it and returned with Louise.

'If I'm in the way or anything just say and I'll clear off.'

'No of course you're not,' Alice said. 'We're just having a snack. Will you join us?'

'Thank you.' Louise accepted a mug of coffee and slice of quiche.

Alice had invited her to be a matron of honour along with Kate, but she'd refused.

'I'm not one for getting done up in dresses and things, you know that. I wouldn't feel comfortable.'

Alice had guessed that wouldn't just be because of the clothes, but didn't say anything else other than, 'OK, but you will come, won't you? And to my hen night?'

'Too right. I'm going to slip something in your drink at the hen night, then turn up at the wedding all innocence to check it's worked.'

'You know, you'd have a better chance of killing me if you didn't keep warning me.'

'Double bluff? Nah, actually I've gone off the idea of killing you. I'm planning to give you something that will create an allergic reaction. You know, scabby skin, boils, hair falling out. That kind of thing.'

'Nice.'

Louise had come to the hen night though and she'd

clinked her glass against Alice's and wished her luck and happiness. True she'd gone home quite early, but she'd done that every time she'd been persuaded to go anywhere with Alice and Hamish.

The two women had made a real effort to become friends and it had worked. Alice hoped it hadn't been too hard for Louise to call and see her shortly before watching her oldest friend marry her newest.

Once they'd all finished eating, Alice's mum told her dad he was in charge of the washing up as he'd not just had his nails done.

'We can redo our lipstick easily enough, but touching up nail varnish never works. Besides, we've got dresses to sort out and it won't take you a minute to get into your suit.'

'No, but it'll take me a while to work out what to do with that cravat thing.'

'It's easy, Dad. I've downloaded a demonstration from YouTube so I'll help you,' Kate said.

'Alice, could I have a quick word before I go?' Louise said.

'Sure. Come through to the lounge.'

They both sat, though in Louise's case perching described it better.

'I... er... here.' She thrust a tiny jewellery box at Alice. Inside was a tiny, polished pale blue stone set into a brooch.

'Thank you, it's beautiful.'

'It's not an actual gemstone or anything. This might seem weird but I found it in the mudflats the day I heard you and Hamish were getting married. Normally of course I'd just leave a stone, but something made me pick it up and keep it. After you asked me to be matron of honour I decided to have it set for you... as your something blue.' Tears dripped down her face.

'Louise, I...'

'Anyway, best be going. See you in church.'

Kate's dress was a simple long shift with a sweetheart neckline, in cream silk. Alice's was made from the same material down to her knees, where it merged into a lace fishtail in the same colour. Her shoulders were bare, but would be covered by the froth of her filmy veil as she walked down the aisle. Both girls wore sashes in the style often used for Scottish weddings, but instead of the family tartan the material was in the same shade of grey-green as Hamish's eyes. Alice pinned the brooch Louise had given her onto her sash. Alice's mum's dress was the same colour as the sashes and so were the ribbon on her hat, and her dad's waistcoat and cravat.

Alice's mobile beeped. There was a text from Louise. 'p.s. It's radioactive'. Alice grinned then switched off her phone. She wouldn't be needing that for some time.

Their mum gave Alice one more tearful hug before Kate dragged her away and into the waiting car, leaving Alice and her dad to wait for its return.

'I've got a surprise for you, love,' he said.

'Oh, thanks, Dad.'

'Be careful not to spill it on your dress though. Beetroot wine can stain something awful, your mum said.'

'Beetroot wine?'

'I saved my last two bottles. One for you today and one for Kate when her time comes.'

'Dad, you really shouldn't have.'

'You'll have a last drink with your dear old dad before you give up his name and take on some other fella's won't you?'

'Put like that, how could I possibly refuse?' She wished it wasn't a rhetorical question and someone would magically appear with an answer.

'I'll just fetch it then.' He looked so happy she knew she'd have to get it down somehow.

She heard a cork pop. Not a good sign as beetroot wine wasn't generally supposed to be sparkling. Oh no! Had it exploded all over him? His dark suit would disguise some of it, but he'd not had the jacket done up. She hurried, as well as her fishtail dress and high heeled shoes allowed, to the kitchen. Her dad was there, pouring champagne into tall glasses and chuckling to himself.

'It seems to have aged pretty well!'

'Dad! That was a mean, rotten trick.'

'It was.' He grinned. 'Don't tell your sister, eh? It'll work just as well on her.'

'OK, I won't.' She accepted her glass and clinked it against her dad's.

They both drank from the glasses he'd poured.

'I can't say anything, love. If I do I'll cry.'

'It's OK, Dad.' She hugged him.

Hamish was waiting for her, wearing a kilt in his family tartan. His brother and Jeff were dressed to match. Hamish had made Jeff his best man.

'No man can be better than the one who carried you out of that fire,' he'd told Alice.

'I'm not so sure about that, but if one of us is going to show our gratitude it's got to be you. No way am I doing any of the things he's suggested. Well, not to him anyway. You might get a demonstration of some of them on our honeymoon.'

As he'd promised, they were spending that back in the cottage in Wales. There would be less hours of daylight than during Alice's first visit there, but neither of them thought that would be a problem.

Alice and Hamish exchanged vows, including the promise to love each other through fire and mud. The new Mr and Mrs Mustarde left church through an archway formed by uniformed firefighters holding up various tools of their trade. Thankfully none of the hoses were connected to a water supply.

The on-duty crew weren't called to a shout, so were able to pop into the reception for a piece of the cake which had been cut with a fireman's axe. Everyone from Red Watch attended with their families including William's new baby daughter. She didn't cry, but Alice's mum did. Again.

'There you are!' Kate said, 'Come on. I've got one matron of honour duty left.' She put her arm through Alice's.

'Where are we going?'

Before Kate could reply, Rachel touched Alice's shoulder.

'Congratulations, Mrs Mustarde.' She kissed Alice's cheek.

'You look really lovely. That's a fabulous dress. The whole thing has been lovely. Thank you so much for inviting us.'

'You're welcome. Thank you both for coming.'

'Congratulations, Alice.' Tony hugged her. She'd not have known which shoulder had been injured had she not seen the damage for herself.

Kate gently tugged her away.

'Where are we going?' Alice asked.

'I have to help you change into your going away outfit.'

'But, I don't... Oi!' She span round to see who'd pinched her bottom. Before she could tell Jeff that rescuing her still wasn't, and never would be, an excuse to do that, Kate interrupted.

'Jeff, shouldn't you be somewhere else?'

'The girls told me to clear off.'

Alice grinned. She'd warned Emma and Lucy about him.

'Well do it then.' Kate gestured to the exit.

'Oh!' He left at speed.

'Thanks. I just hope he doesn't bump into Louise. She's been putting on a brave face, but I don't think she's having a great day.'

'You're kidding? Seen your new brother-in-law lately?'

'No. Where is he?'

'Dunno, but Louise is with him. Donald might look just like his brother, but I think his personality is better suited to Louise.'

'So do I. Where is Hamish? He went off with Devon somewhere and other than Jeff I've not seen any of Red

Watch since. They wouldn't have gone on a shout today, would they?'

'No. Now come on!'

'Kate, you know I haven't got a going away outfit to change into.'

'I know, but it's traditional. I'm probably supposed to tell you about the birds and the bees or something.'

'Ah! Then lead on. This should be good.'

Kate led her up the hotel stairs and into a small bedroom.

'I'd try getting some of the confetti out the front of my dress but people will just throw more when we leave.'

'I expect so.' Kate handed Alice a wrapped gift. 'Devon asked me to give you this.'

'That's sweet of him. Red Watch have already given us a pile of things. I don't think they're all fire extinguishers. This definitely isn't.'

'Go on, open it.'

'I can't do that without Hamish.'

'You can, it's just for you.'

A fire engine shaped gift tag confirmed that. Alice opened the package and found a coil of soft white rope. 'I don't understand.'

'You will in a moment.'

Kate opened the curtains allowing a blue light to fill the room. Alice looked out and saw a fire truck below. The ladder was raised to her window. Hamish, now wearing his uniform trousers, climbed up.

'Mrs Mustarde, woman of my dreams, I want to be the

man in your fantasies.'

He put her over his shoulder, waited for Kate to wrap the rope round Alice's dress to stop it getting snagged on the ladder, and carried her down.

Alice covered his face in kisses as their guests cheered and rained confetti down on them.

Thank you for reading this book. I hope you enjoyed it. If you did, I'd really appreciate it if you could spare the time to leave a short review on Amazon and/or Goodreads.


To learn more about my writing life, hear about new releases and get a free short ebook, news and competitions, sign up to my newsletter – subscribepage.io/ItLSNa or you can find the link on my website patsycollins.co.uk

# About the Author

As well as ten novels, Patsy Collins has had over 500 short stories published, mostly in magazines in the United Kingdom, Ireland, Sweden, Australia and South Africa. Many of these also appear in her themed collections, each containing 24 stories.

She lives in Hampshire with her photographer husband Gary Davies. A lot of their time is spent in their campervan, which they use as a mobile office. Much of Patsy's work is written in the locations at which her stories are set. That was the case with Firestarter, although the van had to double as the cute Welsh cottage and doesn't have a bath big enough for two!

Patsy enjoyed studying the birds and seals mentioned in the book, eating all Alice's favourite food and was absolutely forced to talk to firemen to check a few facts. She's not saying how thorough her research was for the scenes set inside the cottage.

# More books by Patsy Collins

Novels

Escape To The Country
A Year And A Day
Paint Me A Picture
Leave Nothing But Footprints
Acting Like A Killer

Little Mallow cosy mystery series

Disguised Murder and Community Spirit
in Little Mallow
Dependable Friends and Deceitful Neighbours
in Little Mallow
Deadly Words and Innocent Gossip
in Little Mallow

Short Story collections

Perfect Timing
Just A Job
Coffee & Cake
Not A Drop To Drink
A Way With Words
Criminal Intent
Crime In Mind
Making A Move
Days To Remember
A Clean Bill Of Health
Your Good Health

Up The Garden Path
Over The Garden Fence
Through The Garden Gate
In The Garden Air
Beyond The Garden Wall

No Family Secrets
Can't Choose Your Family
Keep It In The Family
Family Feeling
Happy Families

Slightly Spooky Stories I
Slightly Spooky Stories II
Slightly Spooky Stories III
Slightly Spooky Stories IV
Slightly Spooky Stories V


All That Love Stuff
With Love And Kisses
Lots Of Love
Love Is The Answer



Non-fiction


Form Story Idea to Reader:
An accessible guide to writing fiction co-authored
with Rosemary J. Kind


A Year Of Ideas: 365 sets of writing prompts and
exercises